When I Fell for You

By

Candace Shaw

Blurb

Has a wedding planner with a commitment phobia finally found the man to make her fall head over heels in love?

Reagan Richardson loves planning extravagant, classy weddings as the head planner of Precious Moments Events. Though the notion of walking down the aisle has never entered her mind … considering none of her boyfriends have ever lasted long enough thanks to her. However, meeting Dr. Blake Harrison changes all of that in a glance and she finds herself in uncharted territory.

Blake knows all about Reagan's fear of commitment but that doesn't stop him from pursuing the ravishing beauty. Breaking down the wall guarding her heart isn't as easy as he thought but being with Reagan has stirred emotions in him that no other woman ever has. Can he convince her that history isn't going to repeat itself this time around?

Chapter One

"I'll be there at nine sharp, Mrs. Watson." Dr. Blake Harrison checked his watch to verify if that was even possible.

It was just after seven in the morning and patients had begun to call him. Normally, his administrative assistant handled phone calls, but a few patients, such as Mrs. Watson, paid high retainers for exclusive access to him. Luckily it wasn't an emergency, but she was concerned about a mole on her upper arm that had appeared overnight. It was more than likely a wart for this wasn't the first time. She was somewhat of a hypochondriac and called him about anything, including a paper cut once because she was scared it would develop into a staph infection. Once he rules out its nothing serious, Mrs. Watson always keeps the conversation going—offering breakfast or lunch—and brags about her granddaughter who she wants him to meet the next time the young lady is in town. Most times he'd stay if he didn't have another appointment soon after because Mrs. Watson was alone after losing her husband a few years back.

After hanging up, Blake did a couple of lunges and leg stretches, hoping to continue with his morning jog along

1

the beach, but his cell phone rang again blocking out the funky yet classic tunes of The Gap Band in his earbuds. When he'd decided to offer concierge services as an extension of his medical practice last summer, he had no idea it would be a huge hit so fast and expand from Brunswick—where his office was located—to St. Simons Island and the surrounding Georgia islands. He'd hired two more doctors for the practice and another one for part-time concierge services which was now Blake's full-time gig.

After chatting with another patient, he started jogging again at a steady pace and was humming along with the music for ten minutes when it was cut off once more by the ringing of his phone.

Groaning, he figured he'd push the ignore option and send it to voicemail until he saw it was his mother. He always answered when she called unless he had a patient.

"Hello, Mom," he greeted, jogging slowly in place.

"I wanted to catch you before you went on your morning jog."

"Too late. I'm over here on St. Simons."

"Oh ... that's different."

"Yep, wanted a change of scenery. Figured the beach would be peaceful." *But the phone keeps ringing.* "Is everything all right?" he asked with concern. His mother wasn't a morning person.

"Yes, just wanted to thank you again for the healthy heart workshop for my sorority's tea. They had a splendid time on Saturday."

"Happy to help."

"You know Soror Darlene's daughter is such a lovely young woman. Wasn't that nice of her to cater the luncheon for free? She's very giving ... like you. Perhaps you can invite her the next time you go to the homeless shelter. I noticed you had a second helping of her peach cobbler. She used Georgia organic peaches and made the

2

dough from scratch. None of that store-bought, canned fruit filling."

Blake chuckled as he knew where this conversation was going to end up. He was happy with his present life; however, his mother was ready for a daughter-in-law and more grandbabies. His two sisters had married straight out of college and both had two children. He was the oldest, and according to his mother, apparently behind at age thirty-eight. However, life for him had flown by rather fast since graduating from medical school. He'd placed his focus strictly on his career to the point of losing a few good women along the way because he didn't place them first in his life.

He chuckled. "Mother, stop trying to play matchmaker. Yes, she's a lovely woman, but I'm not interested."

"I saw you two chatting and exchanging phone numbers … I thought perhaps—" her voice trailed into a dampened sigh.

"She was asking me about a medical issue for her boyfriend whose phone number she gave me."

"I just want you to settle down with one good woman and stop being such a playboy."

Scrunching his forehead, he pushed the mute button on the phone and let out a long groan. He wasn't a playboy, yet his mother swore he was because while he dated she hadn't met any of the women since his last long-term relationship, which ended over two years ago. Blake didn't see the point of introducing someone to his family unless it was serious.

Unmuting the phone, Blake made sure to not sound frustrated upon speaking. "Mother, you know I'm not a playboy. Nowhere near it. When I meet the one, you will, too."

"Okay, dear. I just want you happy. Finish your jog."

"Love you, Mother."

"Love you, too."

After hanging up, Blake pivoted on his heel and decided to jog back in the direction toward the parking lot of the Coast Guard Station beach where he'd begun. The conversation with his mother filled his thoughts, drowning out the music in his ears. They'd had the same discussion off and on for the past year even though lately it seemed as if it was every time they spoke. At first he assumed there was a medical issue she wasn't disclosing, such as her breast cancer returning. However, his father reassured him that wasn't the case and when it was time for her yearly physical exam, there was nothing amiss.

Blake practically had the beach to himself minus a few other joggers, but it had begun to fill with aerobics and yoga groups now that the sun had fully risen. It was early spring so the island wasn't full of tourists yet, but no doubt with spring break just around the corner followed by Memorial Day that would all change which meant a busy season for him. Last summer—after placing ads at hotels and with the island vacation rental properties—vacationers called him for medical services ranging from simple issues like allergies to diagnosing liver cancer.

Slowing down, Blake placed his focus on the women's yoga class that was in the tree pose position. Their arms were straight up in the air with their hands clasped together. The ladies stood on their right leg as the left leg was bent at the knee with the foot resting on the lower, inner thigh. All of the women were focused and staring ahead at the ocean while soft relaxation music played from a nearby CD player.

One of the participants caught his attention immediately and it wasn't her loud, neon green yoga pants either. Her full, luscious lips, doe-shaped eyes, and cute little nose that graced her gorgeous face caused him to jog backwards to take in the beautiful scene before him. Her thick, jet black hair was pulled up in a messy side ponytail, and her honey-dipped skin glistened, sending his manhood to attention. The slight curve of her supple lips hinted she was aware of his presence yet she continued to stare straight ahead.

As much as he wanted to stand there all day and watch the poised beauty, he realized that wasn't an option when the instructor glanced at him with a stern expression for interrupting her class. Some of the women began to whisper, and a few even slipped off balance from their tree pose, but not the one whose dark, thick eyelashes fluttered over her gaze out to the sea. He mouthed sorry to the instructor and gave a slight nod to the woman who sent his pulse on an adrenaline rush.

Chastising himself for not jogging along the beach sooner, he continued up to a row of benches in front of the parking lot and did a few cool down stretches while his eyes never left the scene before him. Their backs were to him now, but Blake was even more impressed by how the mystery woman's curvy hips and lifted butt rested in her yoga pants.

Checking the time, Blake sighed knowing if he didn't jump in his car at that second, he'd be late for his nine o'clock appointment and he needed to go home to shower. However, when the women changed poses, he sat on a bench and decided to take in the scene for a few more minutes. As The Gap Band's "Outstanding" crept through his earbuds, he had to admit the only woman in his view was indeed outstanding.

*****

"That's right, ladies. Stretch as far as possible and hold your pose," Danielle Sampson instructed to her class of twenty women who struggled to hold their downward dog pose on the bumpy beach sand. She walked in between the ladies, offering assistance and complimenting them. "Doing a great job, Reagan."

"Thanks, Dani."

If we don't change positions soon I'm going to fall flat on my face, Reagan Richardson thought as she kept her eyes focused on the yellow rose on her pink beach towel. Her right hand wasn't lying as flat as possible even though she'd tried to smooth out the sand before laying out the towel. When she'd registered for the beginner's yoga class three weeks ago to relieve stress, she thought surely 'Yoga on the Atlantic' at seven on Monday mornings would be the perfect way. While it had helped with unwinding and starting out her week on a good note, Reagan's mind still drifted to wedding gowns, flower arrangements, cakes, and irritated bridesmaids who weren't happy with the color of their dresses. However, relaxation, being healthy, and staying stress free were her main priorities. Having lost her mother when she was only four years old because of a heart condition, she always feared it could happen to her as well. At age thirty-one, Reagan was a few years shy of the age when her mother had passed, and now that she was growing older, the thought of having the same fate scared her at times.

Exhaling in and out slowly as instructed, her focus was once more intruded by her thought process that wouldn't shut off and had unraveled her for the past few minutes. Reagan couldn't shake the handsome man who had jogged by moments before from her brain. She'd tried to keep her attention straight ahead on the family of dolphins swimming in the ocean while in the uncomfortable tree pose. But when the view was interrupted by the drop-dead gorgeous gentlemen with the amazing smile that jogged backwards just to stare at her, she nearly fell over. However, she didn't want to completely embarrass herself and fall head over heels in front of him. Instead, she stood firm in the sand to keep her balance until he was out of sight and then slipped out of the pose.

He had a lean athletic body with muscles stretching out the fraternity T-shirt and black jogging shorts which weren't doing anything to hide his toned thighs and butt. He wasn't overly tall. She figured right at six-feet which was a nice height in her opinion. Not too short or too tall but just right for her at five-foot-six. She laughed at herself for even being concerned about his height. It wasn't like she would ever date him, but she always preferred to kiss a man without standing on her tippy toes. Yet at the same time be able to rest her head on his chest if barefoot and not topple over him if she wore heels.

Goodness, Reagan wanted to turn in his direction to see where on earth he'd disappeared, but more than likely to the parking lot. She hadn't noticed him before as some of the early morning joggers were familiar to her. He was probably a tourist which meant it was highly unlikely that she'd ever see him again, but at least he'd made her smile for a moment with the amusing backward jog.

"That's it, ladies. Just … a few … more minutes," Dani stammered in a shaky voice. "And then … one … more …"

Reagan wanted to break her pose to peek at Dani because her words were staggered and breathless. She'd only been walking around and assisting; plus, there was a breeze yet she seemed as if she was flushed. Reagan was concerned for her instructor whose summer wedding she was in the process of planning.

As Dani passed her once more, Reagan whispered, "Are you okay?"

"I'll make it. We're almost …"

Dani's voice trailed off as she collapsed right next to Reagan.

"Oh my goodness!" Reagan screeched as she stooped to Dani's side along with the other women. Dani was conscious as she tried to sit up, but fell to the sand once more while mumbling that she was okay.

"Stand back, ladies. I'm a doctor," a man's deep voice commanded as he knelt beside Dani with a black bag, which he immediately opened and pulled a stethoscope out of. Turning his head, he rested dark brown eyes on Reagan. "What's her name?"

Reagan's heart skipped a beat as she realized it was the handsome jogger from earlier but now wasn't the time to be in awe over him. "Danielle. Her name is Danielle."

He placed his attention on Dani as she continued trying to sit up. "No, stay still, Danielle," he said in a calm, soothing voice. "I'm Dr. Harrison and here to help. When was the last time you ate something?"

"Last … night. I was running late this … morning …"

"Are you hyperglycemic?"

"Yes …I thought I'd be okay until after the class."

"Does anyone have any snacks or fruit in their tote bags?" he asked, glancing around.

One of the women scurried to her bag, unpeeled a banana, and handed it to Dani.

Reagan held Dani's hand and spoke encouraging words while Dr. Harrison tested a prick of blood from her finger with a blood sugar tester.

"Yep, its low. Do you have any other health issues I need to know about?" he inquired, checking her temperature with an ear thermometer and then her pulse as she snacked on the fruit.

"No. No. Usually I'm on top of this, but lately I've been busy with adding on more yoga classes and stressing over my upcoming wedding."

"Well, I understand. However, your health is very important. I'm sure your future husband will agree."

Dani gave a half smile and a nod. "Yeah, he would."

"I suggest resting if possible for the rest of the morning and eat a full meal. Do you have someone to drive you home?"

"I will," Reagan volunteered.

He turned to Reagan once more, but this time instead of the concernment for Dani, it was replaced with the intriguing stare he'd presented earlier to her. A smile smoothed across his chiseled face and Reagan couldn't help but smile back almost on demand. The man had ruffled her feathers, causing her to not be able to concentrate because she'd had an inkling he was still somewhere nearby checking her out. Apparently, her assumption was correct, and she was grateful he could help Dani.

They both stood at the same time while some of the ladies continued to comfort their instructor.

"Perfect … um … Ms. …?" He held out his hand to her as his eyes gripped onto hers tight.

For a moment, she was oblivious to her surroundings as his intense gaze held her in a hypnotic state as if he was waving a pocket watch in front of her. "I'm Reagan …" She paused, sliding her right hand into his while concentrating to keep her voice steady. His palm was warm. Comforting. Almost familiar, as if he'd caressed her body before, and a burning sensation washed over her skin at the erotic thought. "Reagan Richardson."

A knowing smile inched up his left jaw. "Ah, *you're* Reagan Richardson."

He squeezed her hand before letting it go. Her normal reaction would be to shove them in her pockets, but unfortunately her yoga pants didn't have any, so she clasped them in front of her. Heat penetrated Reagan's cheeks and a gulp wedged in her throat, but luckily she sounded normal upon speaking.

"You act as if we know each other." *Trust me, I would have remembered meeting a handsome man like you.*

"We spoke briefly over the phone once. Zaria Braxton planned my New Year's Eve Bash. Her husband, Garrett, is one of the partners at my practice."

"Oh, *you're* Blake Harrison," she realized, remembering she did speak with him pertaining to the rules for the massive fireworks display he wanted to have at the party. "Zaria and Garrett always speak very highly of you. I heard the party was a success."

"It was over the top. Zaria did far more than I expected."

"Of course. Precious Moments Events is first-class every time." A nervous sensation rippled through her body at his closeness and she stepped back. Men rarely made her nervous, even the drop-dead handsome ones like Blake, yet there was something enduring about him.

"Well, I may need one of you to plan my parents' 40th wedding anniversary. My sisters and I are, but … um, I think we could use some professional reinforcements."

"No problem. We can do that." She glanced over at Dani who was breathing easy again and chatting with the ladies. "Well, thank you for helping Dani. I'm going to whisk her home now."

Reagan noted a solemn, reluctant expression cascade over his face as if he wanted to continue chatting and it tugged at her because she didn't want to leave either.

Reaching into his back pocket, Blake pulled out his wallet and sifted through it until he slid out a business card. "If you ever need any medical concierge services, I'm your man."

The thought of a coughing fit on the spot crossed her mind, but she shoved it aside. However, the way he said 'I'm your man' had her envisioning him as such, causing her to remember Zaria stating that when you meet a man you'll know within the first five minutes whether you only like him for a friend, to date, just sex, or more. This was the first time Reagan thought of more and her skin prickled with tiny goose bumps.

"Thank you, Dr. Harrison."

He ran a sultry gaze over her once more, and hesitated as if he wanted to say something else but changed his mind. "Nice meeting you, Reagan."

After he checked on Dani, said good-bye to the ladies, and strolled to the parking lot, Reagan was able to breathe again.

*****

Blake read over the blood test results from a patient who'd had slightly high cholesterol and was relieved that the levels were back to normal. Thanks to changing his diet and exercise without the need of medication, Blake hoped that the patient would stick to the regiment considering his wife was ill and had been overcome with worry. Picking up the phone, he called with the good news and promised to stop by their home later that week.

Checking his watch, he realized he had a few more minutes before he had to leave for his next appointment at noon with a patient on Jekyll Island. Closing his eyes for a moment, Blake was transported back to earlier that morning and meeting the lovely Reagan Richardson. He hated like hell that he couldn't stick around longer to chat with her and was even more upset that he'd didn't ask for her private number, but he understood she needed to take her friend home. He'd found a number on the Precious Moment's website for her, but when he called a voicemail greeting with another woman's voice stated they were closed. He didn't bother leaving a message considering it was a business number, and while he did want her to assist with his parents' dinner party, he didn't want to discuss business with her. He wanted to ask her out and not over a voicemail that more than just her had access to.

He figured he could jog by again next week to see her, but a week was too long of a time to wait. By then some other man could've met her, asked her out, and she'd fallen in love by then. Nope, that couldn't happen.

Scooting his chair away from his desk, Blake headed toward the door and across the hall to Dr. Garrett Braxton's office.

"Hey, man," Blake greeted, leaning on the door jamb. "You have a minute?"

Garrett nodded as he sipped his coffee and motioned for Blake to sit in the brown leather chair in front of his desk. "I have a patient waiting in the exam room but Jessica is with him at the moment drawing blood." He closed a file he was reading over. "What's up?"

Blake shut the door and slammed into the chair, noticing that Garrett had cut his fro down to a low fade since he last saw him on Friday.

"I met Zaria's cousin, Reagan, this morning. Why haven't you introduced me to her? She's the most beautiful woman I ever laid eyes on."

Garrett's eyebrows rose along with a sly grin. "Ah ... I see." Crossing his hands on the desk, he leaned toward his friend. "That would explain the extra bounce in your step when you arrived earlier."

"What do you know about her? Is she seeing anyone? I checked her ring finger so I'm assuming she's not engaged. I'm not one for stealing someone's woman, but she's the type that's making a brother give it some thought."

"You're in luck," Garrett joked. "She's single, but ..."

"But what? She's a psycho?" he asked, slapping his knee. "Damn. Maybe I could overlook that this one time."

"No. She's a sweetheart, but has a habit of dumping men early in the relationship. I don't think any man has lasted longer than six months with her."

"That's because she hadn't met me yet."

"Zaria thinks it's because Reagan's father left her mother right before Reagan was born and has daddy abandonment issues. He's barely in her life now. I think she's scared of being hurt and breaks up with them before they break up with her. But hey, maybe you'll be the one to make her fall. If not, you can always date Mrs. Watson's granddaughter, or worse ...someone on your mother's list." Garrett cracked a sarcastic smile.

"Don't remind me. I had the pleasure of seeing more pictures of the granddaughter today over breakfast. She's cute, but I'm not interested. Anything else about Reagan?"

"She can cook. Remember the office Christmas party and Zaria brought the Shepherd's pie? Reagan baked it."

"Mmm ... it was delicious. I do love a woman that can throw down in the kitchen."

"So are you going to ask her out?"

"I didn't ask for her number ..." he said, kicking himself for that misstep.

"You're slipping, bro. Reagan has a new number, and I don't have it yet. Just call Zaria." Checking his watch, Garrett stood and swiped his white coat from the back of his chair. "They're together right now for their weekly brunch meeting. I'm sure she won't mind. She's always saying how she wants Reagan to find a good man."

"I'll do that before I leave for Jekyll." Standing, Blake headed toward the door with Garrett. "Thanks, man."

"No problem. I'll give Zaria a heads up. Let me know if Reagan says yes."

Blake frowned as he opened the door and stepped into the hall. "If? You mean *when* she says yes."

"Haven't heard you talk like this in a long while about a woman."

"Hadn't met the one yet."

Chapter Two

Reagan perused her notes for the weekly Precious Moments Events' brunch meeting at her home that also served as their place of business. She always held the meeting on her veranda on beautiful, sunny days so her eyes could escape to the fascinating blue water of the Atlantic Ocean that was her backdrop and a reminder of how hard she'd worked to make her dream come true.

She tried to focus on her best friend and business partner Brooklyn Vincent's ideas about the photography for an upcoming wedding weekend of festivities. However, Reagan's thoughts continued to sway to earlier that morning and meeting the handsome hunk, Blake Harrison. She couldn't believe that her brain wouldn't shut off thinking about him. His warm smile and the lips that produced it were inviting and succulent. It had taken everything in her not to trace her finger along the sexy curve of them. Blake's caramel-coated skin seemed almost too perfect to belong to a man, for it was baby smooth and supple. When he spoke, his deep voice had caressed her body like a hot wave of ecstasy, and it was still coated with tingling sensations that hadn't vanished even after a shower.

Sipping her black coffee only reminded her of Blake's dark, smoldering gaze that had bore into her when they'd first laid eyes on each other. She didn't believe in love at first sight, but there had been an emotion that jolted through her that she couldn't explain. She chalked it up to he was an attractive man and what woman's bottom lip wouldn't drop down to the beach sand in awe?

Struggling to halt this nonsense about Blake, she placed her attention on Zaria as she discussed her vision for an upcoming event. The words were on the tip of Reagan's tongue to inform Zaria about meeting Blake. However, she knew her cousin would start playing match maker considering she'd hinted once that she would love to introduce them. Though now Reagan couldn't shake him out of her head. It wreaked havoc on her concentration and cooking skills. Little did her co-planners know the batch of pancakes they were eating was the third one. The other two were sitting burnt in the outside garbage can because she'd neglected them while she'd researched Blake on the Internet.

Unfortunately, there wasn't much about him on the world wide web. Just his medical practice website that had a jaw-dropping picture of him on his bio page which caused her to burn the first batch. The second batch of pancakes joined the first as she'd read about a scholarship fundraiser gala he'd attended and there was also a picture of him posing with the teenagers who were receiving scholarships. He was debonair in his tuxedo and oozed sex appeal. Realizing she was almost out of blueberries and couldn't burn anymore pancakes, she had closed the laptop, hoping to shut out thoughts of the dreamy doctor.

"Reagan, is there anything else you would like to contribute to today's meeting that you have not been a part of?" Zaria asked sarcastically, sliding the diamond 'Z' back and forth on her necklace. It was a Christmas gift from her husband years ago and she rarely took it off. "You seem spaced out."

Swiping her hand through her loose, back-length curls, Reagan smiled innocently. "Girl, I'm fine," she answered, knowing that was a lie. "I was just thinking about Dani. She got light-headed in the middle of our yoga session this morning."

"Poor thing. I know she's stressed out over her upcoming nuptials," Addison Arrington, the newest member of their event planning team stated with concern.

"Yep. Its pre-wedding jitters and not eating like she's supposed to." Reagan stood with her empty plate and grabbed the other ones. "Today's meeting went well. Zaria, can you check with the conference center on Jekyll Island and see if they have another meeting room available for the teacher's convention?"

"I'll take care of that now …" Zaria paused as her cell phone vibrated in her hand. Frowning, she eyed the screen for a moment. "Dr. Harrison? Perhaps we're about to add a new event, ladies."

Reagan's heart raced at the sound of his name and the plates in her hands began to rattle. Catching Addison's inquisitive stare, she forced her hands to stop shaking, but it only sped up her pulse which she had no control over.

Pushing the button on the screen, Zaria answered with a professional hello. "Oh… Okay… Sure. Reagan is right here." A confused expression washed over Zaria's face as she handed Reagan the phone.

Placing the plates back on the table, she breathed deep before speaking.

"Hello, Dr. Harrison." *Whew. That sounded steady. I think. They're all staring as if I have antlers growing out of my head.*

"Hey, Reagan. After I rushed off, I realized that I never got either of your information. I wanted to check on Danielle."

Right. Of course. It's not like he's calling to ask me out. "Oh, she's doing better. I stayed with her while she ate breakfast and her fiancée came over to check on her as well."

"Great. Great." Pausing, he hesitated and cleared his throat. "The other reason why I'm calling is … I can't stop thinking about you."

An unexpected gasp slipped out and her heart banged hard against her chest until it hurt. The serious yet seductive tone of his words sprinkled prickles over her body. Did she hear him correctly? The man who had clouded her brain since the second he'd jogged by couldn't stop thinking about her. She swore she was lost in one of the romance novels she'd recently read.

"Oh really?"

"I would love to get to know you better on a date."

"A date?" she asked a little too loudly as three sets of eyes widened.

Addison began to mouth yes over and over while the other two followed suit. Zaria placed her head against the back of the phone to listen in on the conversation, but Reagan scooted away as her cousin smacked her lips.

"Can I think about it and get back to you?"

"Sure," he answered in an upbeat manner. "My cell number is on the card I gave you."

"I'll let you know, and I'll inform Dani that you called to check on her."

"Perfect. I look forward to hearing from you, and hopefully seeing you again. Soon."

"Good-bye, Blake."

"Good-bye, beautiful."

Handing the phone back to Zaria, Reagan grabbed the dishes, darted inside, and straight to the kitchen with her girls on her heel. The heat rushing to her cheeks burned as she tried her damnedest to hold in the smile that wanted to burst through. *Did Dr. Dreamy really just ask me out? And why the heck didn't I shout yes immediately when he asked?*

"Neglect to tell us something?" Zaria asked in her usual sassy tone. "Perhaps that's why you were in la la land during brunch."

"He was present when Dani fainted and he assisted. That's all."

Brooklyn twisted her lips into a smirk. "No, that is definitely not all."

"Yeah, he's asking you out. Mmm-hmm," Zaria said, placing her hands on her hips. "You must've made an impression on him. Were you wearing your neon green yoga pants?"

"What's there to think about?" Addison interjected, taking the plates from Reagan and beginning to set them in the dishwasher. "I met him once at an event. He's super hot! The ladies couldn't keep their eyes off of him."

Reagan chuckled at Addison, who at twenty-five was the youngest and the most daring of the friends. Her fiery red hair, vintage style of dress, and outgoing personality always had a lasting impression on anyone she met. She didn't grow up with the other ladies but had fit right in when Reagan's sister-in-law recommended her baby cousin to join their team after she graduated from college.

"I don't know if I'm ready to go out with anyone." Reagan put up her hand in a halting gesture. "And no, I'm not hung up on my ex. It's been over six months. However, I still feel like I'm in limbo. The dates I've been on lately have had no chemistry. While Blake seems like a nice guy, I don't see the point of wasting my time. Besides, he wants me to plan his parent's anniversary party. There's a conflict of interest. You know we don't date clients."

"Girl, I can plan the party," Zaria offered, opening the refrigerator and pulling out a bottled water. "Give me another excuse."

"It's just one date," Brooklyn reminded in a comforting tone. "We're not saying marry the man tomorrow. But the expression on your face when you realized who was calling for you ... well, let's just say as a photographer, I study people's facial expressions. Yours spoke volumes, my friend."

Zaria flipped her waist-length hair away from her face to take a swig of the water. "Heck, her face spoke volumes ever since we arrived and now we know why. Reagan was daydreaming about Blake Harrison. Seems like your daydream may become a reality." She set the water bottle down on the counter and grabbed her cell phone.

Sighing deep, Reagan knew she couldn't squirm her way out of this especially with Zaria. "I'll give it some thought, but I'm not promising a yes. Just some thought."

"Uh huh," Zaria mumbled under her breath as she typed on her cell phone. "I'm texting him your cell number right now."

"Gee, thanks," Reagan said through a clenched smile.

"Anytime …" Zaria's voice drifted off as she tilted her head to the side. "So, I just received a text message from my husband. It says: 'Heads up, Z. Blake is going to call you soon. He's met Reagan and I think the brother has fallen hard already. He wants to ask her out.' Now G tells me?"

*****

Later on that night, Reagan relaxed on the chaise lounge in her bedroom with a mug of green tea and her cell phone seated on the pillow next to her. Under the phone was Blake's business card. She'd toiled on her decision the entire day, and now that she'd made up her mind, it was time to inform Blake.

Reagan jumped when the shrill of her phone sounded and she glanced at the screen to see the picture of her big brother Justin that was saved on her phone. She couldn't help but laugh every time his photo of mostly wild, curly hair graced her screen. He'd considered cutting it but his wife loved the craziness of it. Sighing in relief of the prolonging of her decision to call Blake, she answered the phone with a cheery hello.

"Hey, baby sis. Busy?"

She could hear a slight frustration in his tone and only two situations ruffled his feathers. A recipe not turning out right or their father … or rather the man they called Mr. Brown because he didn't deserve the title of dad or father. Lately, he'd reached out to Justin, who he shared a first name with, a few times only to still be a disappointment. Their father hadn't been in their lives much since her parents had finally ended their on/off again relationship two months before Reagan was born. She didn't have many memories of her mother, yet Justin—who was twelve at the time—had taken her death very hard and hated their father more than he cared to admit for deserting them. For Reagan, their maternal grandparents who'd raised them had been her true parents, but there were times when she'd longed to know her real parents, especially her mother.

"No. What's wrong?"

"Well … I just got off the phone with Mr. Brown."

So it's the latter. "Oh." Was all she could muster up in a who-cares tone. She'd tried over the years to be close with her dad. She'd always thought it would be cool to be a daddy's girl like Zaria was with her father. But as she grew older, it no longer bothered Reagan that he wasn't a permanent staple in her life and she'd gotten used to their situation. Her grandparents had been wonderful parents to her before they'd passed away three years ago a couple of months apart and she was grateful to them.

Justin chuckled sarcastically at her remark. "Yeah … that was my same exact sentiment when I heard his voice on the other end. Anyway, he's back in Memphis, or probably never left and wants to stop by the restaurant to see me."

"Mmm …sounds like he wants something."

A rush of air from Justin filled her ears and for a moment she felt sorry for her big brother who she knew deep down had always wanted a father/son relationship. Luckily, he had that type of relationship with his own son and father-in-law.

"Probably. That's usually how it works with him."

"What did you tell him?"

"Sure. Why not? He's not going to show."

"I know. Wouldn't be the first time."

Reagan's memory jolted to the time when Justin decided to invite their father to his wedding but he was a no-show with the excuse that he'd missed his plane. A friend of the family mentioned to Reagan that she spotted him two days later playing Black Jack in a casino in Tunica, Mississippi which was an hour from Memphis.

"Anyway, enough about him. How was your weekly brunch meeting with the ladies? Did you use my recipe for the veggie quiche?"

"Yes, and it was a big hit. I put my on twist on it by topping it with feta cheese and diced tomatoes." Luckily, she didn't burn it during her research session because she only had enough to make it once.

"Oh, boy," he said in a teasing manner. "Here we go. Experimenting with my recipes."

"You may own one of the most popular dinner and blues clubs in Memphis, but it doesn't mean you're the only chef in the family."

"I know. You remind me all the time."

"Whatever. How's Shelbi?"

"She's doing well. Ready for the baby to arrive."

"Just three more months! I'm excited to meet my niece. I bet little Jay can't wait to be a big brother. I'm sure he's going to be overprotective of Shelbi's mini me just like you are of me."

"He better be. Speaking of … anyone I need to meet or know about?"

Was he a freaking mind reader or had he spoken to Zaria. "Oh … uh … nope."

"I'll take that as a yes."

"Relax, Jay. We haven't been on a first date yet."

"Mmm … okay. Just checking. Take your mace if you go."

"I don't have any mace, but Addison and I did take a kickboxing class."

"Even better. Aim where it will hurt the most."

"You're crazy. Kiss the family for me. I'll talk to you later."

After hanging up, she stared at the cell phone in her hand and the business card perched on the pillow. Letting out a long exhale, she dialed Blake's number and rested her head against the back of the chaise as her heart raced loud enough for him to probably hear.

"Hello," he answered in a professional tone. "This is Dr. Harrison."

His voice sent a ripple of goose bumps along her arms. Even over the phone he unraveled her. "Hi. It's Reagan Richardson."

"Why, hello there."

His manner changed from professional to sexy and a gulp rested like a big lump in Reagan's throat. She imagined his alluring smile glide across his ruggedly handsome face, and she hated the fact that she was easily turned on by his charisma over the phone.

"I hope you're calling with a yes?"

"Um …yes and no. It's not that I don't want to, but in perusing my schedule for the next few weeks, my weekends are full with events. Not sure how long you'd want to wait for a date."

"Soooooooo … you don't go out on week nights, or is this your way of telling me no as nicely as possible?"

"No, it's not that. I do have a few week nights that I work. Rehearsal dinners and what not."

"What are you doing tomorrow evening?"

"Glassblowing session."

"That's the most creative no I've ever heard. You could've just said washing your hair."

She found his sarcastic humor rather amusing. "Laughing out loud, Blake. I'm serious. My good friend

Kameryn Monroe is a glass sculptor. She has a workshop that I signed up for."

"Ah, yes. I saw her exhibit at the Brunswick Art Gallery last year. Very beautiful and unique sculptures. Making one sounds like fun yet difficult at the same time."

"I know, right? I've watched her plenty of times and she makes it seem so easy. You're welcome to join me."

"Cool. What time do you want me to pick you up?"

"I'll meet you there. I have a meeting with her beforehand. She's making vases for an upcoming event. But the class starts at 7:00 p.m. at her studio in downtown Brunswick. I'll text you the information."

"Perfect. I look forward to seeing you for our first date."

"Date? I wouldn't really consider it a date. How about we call it an outing and get to know each other?"

He chuckled. "Well, whatever you want to call it, I look forward to the workshop, but most importantly learning more about the beautiful woman I can't wait to see."

"Can't wait."

"Until tomorrow evening."

After pressing end on the phone, Reagan scrolled through her contacts until she found Zaria's name and pressed it.

"Hola, chica," Zaria greeted in an upbeat manner. "Did you make a decision or do you need some advice?"

"No. I called him back. We're going out tomorrow evening."

"That was fast. Garrett said Blake is smitten with you. We're ecstatic. We can double date."

"Slow down, Z. He may not make it past the first date."

"I forgot about you and your pickiness."

Reagan could easily imagine Zaria smacking her lips and rolling her eyes at the end of her statement. "I'm not picky," Reagan reminded despite the fact that she knew it was a lie. "Just careful. I don't want to end up like my mother with a man who doesn't respect me."

"And you won't," Zaria said with reassurance. "But the way you keep dumping brothers, you'll never find Mr. Right. Instead, you're going to end up an old maid with five cats."

Reagan sighed and almost regretted calling. "Here we go again."

"I'll stop talking about it when I begin to plan your wedding. Anyway, where are you going?"

"I invited him to Kam's glassblowing workshop."

"That's unique. So what's up?"

"Tell me everything you know about Blake. One of the reasons I said yes is that you and your husband know him."

"I don't know that much. That's for you to find out. But let me see. He's from a prominent family … sort of like the Arringtons. His dad is some big time ranking military man who worked at the Pentagon for years and his mom used to be a fashion editor for *Grace and Style Magazine*. I met her while working on his New Year's Eve party. She'd like you. From what I've witnessed, Dr. Harrison is very down to earth, he loves to deep sea fish, and water sports. He conducts healthy heart workshops which is perfect since you're into that type of thing."

"He's not a player, is he?"

"No. Garrett said Blake dates but his prime focus has always been his medical practice."

"Anything else?"

"Just be you and have fun."

"I can do that."

"Good. Now I'm going to go play 'doctor' with my husband. Perhaps you'll be doing the same soon with your doctor."

"One step at a time, Z."

"Girl, it's been ages since you played doctor, and I'm not talking about your special friend that needs batteries."

Reagan chuckled at Zaria who was never afraid to talk about sex. "I'm hanging up now."

After clicking off the call, she headed toward her bed as she thought about her date the next evening. She was overcome with giddiness as Blake's handsome face and deep, sensual voice entered her mind. She felt like a teenager who was going on her very first date with the most popular guy in the school. Anxiousness swept over her at the notion that there was something different about her attraction to Blake. She'd had a few serious relationships, gone on numerous dates, and dated without the title of boyfriend. While her family and friends concluded she was picky and had daddy issues, Reagan chalked it up to simply knowing that none of those guys had been the one. She didn't miss any of them, had never fallen in love, and knew when the relationship wouldn't lead to marriage. However, now a serene presence and awareness of something new was in her midst, and it all started that morning when Blake smiled at her and she nearly fell over.

*****

Blake strolled into the industrial building's lobby, which was decked out with a variety of unique shaped glass art. A few people were there chatting and admiring the creative pieces. Some of the sculptures sat on the floor, and a few pointy and medusa-wiggly ones hung from the ceiling draped with tiny white lights, while other eccentric ones flanked shelves or graced the walls. It was an amazing sight, and he was in awe of the vibrant colors and masterpieces until a delicate, engaging scent filled his atmosphere and outshone the magnificent surroundings.

A knowing grin reached his lips as he pivoted and landed his stare on the lady gliding toward him. A wide smile that he sensed was created just for him enhanced her high cheek bones and deepened the dimple on her right cheek. Midnight curls were swept back from her face with a purple hairband matching the flared dress that stopped

just below the knees. Toned, soft legs were encased in flat black gladiator-type sandals that wrapped the bottom of her calves. The image of her in neon yoga pants and tennis shoes had filled his thoughts since meeting her. Now, she was even more whimsical and delightful than he remembered, especially when she flashed another alluring smile that raced his pulse to 120 miles per hour in one second flat.

Reagan gave him a warm hug and her scent engulfed him even more into her essence. Sliding his hands around her waist, he pulled her closer against him and her body fit snug in his arms. He didn't want to be too forward, but at the same time there was something about her so familiar and surreal as if she was right where she belonged. With him. While that excited him it also scared him for he'd never experienced a connection with a woman this fast unless it was a lustful feeling and that hadn't crept into his mind.

"Hey there," he greeted, reluctantly stepping back as she slipped out of his embrace and shoved her hands in the side pockets of her pleated dress.

"Hey, Blake. I hope you weren't waiting long. Kameryn and I just finished our meeting."

"Nope. Just walked in. I was admiring all of the glass art."

"Isn't it creative?" She picked up a scalloped-shape blue and purple swirled bowl. "I wouldn't mind trying something like this tonight. I need a centerpiece for my kitchen table. Aren't they the most beautiful pieces of art you've ever seen?" Setting the dish back, she wandered to a rainbow swirled floor vase in the corner. "This is neat, too."

"While they're all beautiful, honestly the most beautiful art I've ever seen is standing in front of me," he stated in a low, serious voice.

Reagan's lips parted into a giggle and the hue on her face changed to a rosy pink. "Thank you," she answered, turning her head away momentarily before resting her eyes back on him. "That's a sweet compliment."

"Just speaking the truth. Why do you think I jogged backwards when I first saw you? I had to do a double take of the woman who nearly caused me to trip over my own feet."

"Mmm ... I did notice a slight stumble." She continued to peruse the shelves with him following. Glancing at him over her shoulder, she stated, "Glad to know I'm the reason. I just thought you were clumsy or had no swag." She shrugged her shoulder, followed by a joking wink.

Blake laughed loud as all the eyes in the room turned their way. He was ecstatic that she was more than a pretty face. Reagan's wit and sarcasm added a layer to her that he appreciated and wanted to learn more about.

"Are you saying I lost some cool points?"

"A few, but you gained them back by helping Danielle. She told me to tell you thank you again."

"I'm glad I decided to stay and admire the view."

"The ocean is peaceful in the morning."

"Mmm-hmm. Hadn't noticed."

She released another gorgeous smile and turned her head away from his.

"You don't want me to see you blush ... again?"

She turned toward him with a straight face even though he could tell she was suppressing a smile. "Nope."

"Hello, everyone," an upbeat female's voice sounded behind them. "Are you all ready to learn how to be a glass sculptor?"

Blake turned around to see Kameryn Monroe standing in the middle of the small crowd wearing a pair of black skinny jeans and a T-shirt with a glass chandelier sculpture printed on it. Her braided hair was wrapped around her head like a crown and her arms were quite toned which he assumed was because of all the spinning and heavy lifting when creating her infamous glass art. While he didn't know her personally, he was familiar with her cousin

Steven Monroe who was the US Senator for the state of Georgia.

Everyone said yes and followed her down a hallway that was laden with pictures of Kameryn and her team making her creations, as well as photos of her art on display at museums, homes, gardens, and centerpieces at events. They arrived inside of a huge factory-type room with concrete floors and exposed piping on the ceiling. There were a few tall tables and stools around the perimeter. Along the front wall were four huge kilns, and on a long table on the opposite wall contained a variety of paints and sand to make the glass.

Reagan selected a workstation near the back of the room and away from the hot kilns. As he pulled out her chair, she nodded a thank you.

"Aren't you a gentleman," Reagan whispered. "I like that."

He sat next to her and leaned over to her ear, hoping the two older ladies behind them wouldn't hear. "I can be whatever you want." His tongue lightly flicked her ear by mistake, causing her to bite her lip.

"Mmm-hmm. I like that, too."

Chapter Three

"That was fun," Blake commented as they strolled to the parking lot carrying tote bags that contained their wrapped matching bowls three hours later. "Definitely a different kind of evening."

"It was. I've witnessed Kam create fascinating objects and sculptures, but to actually experience it? I honestly didn't think I could handle pulling it out of the fire and spinning it into a spectacular bowl. And thank you for your help. I almost dropped it," she laughed. "Twice."

"I would've given you mine. I know you wanted something for your table."

"That's nice of you. Are you always so giving, or is this just first date niceness that will wear off by the fifth one?" she asked jokingly.

"Again, Reagan, I'll be whatever you want me to be."

Her face flushed at the thought of finding out. She couldn't even believe she'd flirted back when he'd said it earlier. Normally a man she barely knew flirting with her was a major turn off, but with him she welcomed it.

"You're a bad boy," Reagan teased as they stopped in front of her car. Popping the trunk of her black Mercedes coupe, she placed her tote bag inside of it. "You just don't know how to quit."

"Didn't you say that's what you like?" he asked in a deep, serious voice. "Just giving the woman what she wants."

The heat in Reagan's cheeks turned up higher than the brightest star in the universe. She couldn't believe she was flirting with Blake, but there was something about him that was easy going and calming. He possessed a sexy swag that was intriguing and unraveled her defenses. Perhaps it was because she hadn't been on a date in ages with a man that she wanted to see again, or perhaps because she hadn't had sex in a long while. She decided to blame it on both until he moved into her personal space, and his smoldering stare burned into her, causing a heat wave to rush over her body.

Nope, I'll blame it on his parents for creating such a fine, intelligent hunk of a man.

Clearing her throat, she stared up at him and decided to change the subject before she suggested he follow her back to her place.

"How about we grab some ice cream?" *Because we both could use a cool down.*

His lips raised in a curious gesture up the left side of his cheek. "Is that your way of saying you want to go back to my place?"

"Um … no," she replied, shaking her head and grabbing his tote bag. She placed it next to hers and shut the trunk. Interlocking her arm with his, Reagan began to walk them back toward the street. "I wasn't referring to sex. I really mean let's grab some ice cream. There's a shop on the other side of Kam's studio. It's the perfect way to cool down after being subjected to over 1000 degrees of glassblowing."

Chuckling, Blake nodded his head in understanding. "I was just teasing. Not saying I haven't had sex on a first date, but I'm not aiming for a casual sexual relationship and that's usually how those end up."

"That is so true."

His eyebrows drew together. "You know from experience as well?" he asked as they turned the corner and stopped on the sidewalk in front of the ice cream shop.

"Yep. I had two relationships like that. One ended up just being a one-time tryst, and the other I tried to make a real relationship out of but we had no chemistry outside of the bedroom. In fact, there were times when that wasn't even the case and we eventually stopped calling each other for hook-ups. I saw him with another woman a month later and felt no emotion whatsoever. Complete waste of my time."

"You know most women don't admit to a one-night stand."

"I'm too old for games and telling tales like my grandmother used to say. I like to be upfront."

"That's good to know." Opening the door, he let her pass through the shop that was crowded with teenagers and a few people from the glass blowing session. "How about we sit outside?" he suggested, pointing his head to the empty row of benches.

"Great idea. I'm sure it's quieter."

After ordering their waffle ice cream bowls, they retreated to a bench a few feet from the shop that had a view of the Sidney Lanier Bridge.

"This is good," Blake commented on his coffee ice cream topped with pecans and chocolate syrup. "No toppings for you, huh?"

"Nope. Just plain, fat-free vanilla bean ice cream. I try to watch what I eat, but every now and then I do indulge in a few of my favorite things."

"Maybe next time we can go out to eat. Do you like French cuisine?"

"I do, but who said I was going out with you again?" she joked, followed by a wink. She definitely wanted to go out with him again and again.

"You did. Apparently, I'm promised at least five dates," Blake reminded with a teasing smirk. "And you're no longer calling this an outing so I guess somewhere along the way I changed your mind. It's an official first date, pretty lady."

She swished her lips to the side. "You're funny. They're just words."

Blake rubbed his chin as a know-it-all expression crossed his face. "May I point out interchangeable words."

Shaking her head, Reagan decided to downplay his comment. "What constitutes a true date? Why can't people just hang out and get to know each other? I've been on first even third dates that were awkward and boring. Tonight hanging with you was fun because I was able to think of it as not a date. I've just been myself." *Must call and thank Zaria for her idea or maybe not. She may start planning my wedding.*

"Obviously you were going out with the wrong men."

"Mmm … maybe. Or perhaps I was expecting the awkwardness or feeling the need to be uptight and on guard instead of just being me."

"You're right, this hasn't been like my dates where I'm searching for the right words to say or making sure I don't say the wrong thing. I've been able to be myself."

Blake took a big spoonful of his ice cream, which had to begun to melt, and a little bit of it ended up on the corner of his bottom lip. Reagan's mouth watered as she stared at the delectable sight. "You have a little ice cream right there." She pointed at the spot she wanted to lick but instead swiped the napkin from her lap and dabbed the ice cream off.

"Thank you." A sly, cocky smile eased across his mouth. "I was wondering why you were staring so hard.

Thought perhaps you were going to kiss me." He winked and proceeded to finish.

Something like that. "Uh … no."

"The night isn't over with," he stated matter-of-factly. "So how many dates do you usually give a brother before deciding he's not the one for you?"

"Just depends. I think in general both parties tend to know within the first few dates if it's going to end up being just friendship, a real relationship, or no need to waste each other's time."

"You have a point." He scooted closer to her. "Soooooo do you want to go on another *outing* with me?"

"I'd like that," Reagan replied honestly. "I have a wedding this Saturday, but I'm free Sunday." She couldn't believe she was giving up her only day off. Sunday's were reserved for alone time, lounging in pajamas, cleaning her home, and preparing for the week.

"Me too. What do you want to do?"

"Mmm … doesn't matter. We can just hang out."

"Oh yes, of course. We can hang out," he said in a teasing manner. "By the way, I told my mother about you."

She nearly choked on the ice cream going down her throat. "Wait. What?"

"Calm down, Reagan. I'm referring to my parents' anniversary party. She'd love to meet with you."

"I assumed you and you were sisters were planning it, not your mother."

"We're paying for it, but my mother … well, let's just say she wants to be involved in the planning. However, what she doesn't know is that my dad is surprising her with a vow renewal. They never had a true wedding. He was in the Army, and they eloped two days prior to him being stationed in Hawaii for four years. He didn't want to go without her."

"How romantic."

"My grandparents didn't think so but they got over it."

"I'll be more than happy to assist, and of course your dad's surprise will be kept a secret. I've done surprise renewals before. I'll need to work out the details, so at some point I'll need to meet with him as well."

"Great. So, tell me how you ended up on St. Simons of all places. Garrett mentioned you all were from Memphis. Why did you choose here to set up a business?"

"I was working for an event planning firm in Atlanta, and I had a destination wedding that was located on the island for a couple who met here on spring break. I instantly fell in love with the scenery and the laid-back feel. I spent three months traveling back and forth with the bride and her family. I connected with a lot of people, and after the wedding, I received requests from locals who attended to plan their weddings or other social events. I took a chance, emptied my savings, and here I am. A year later, Zaria and Brooklyn joined me. We'd always joked about opening our own event planning company someday so I was elated when they immediately said yes. Last summer we added another planner who is a family friend from Memphis."

"Cool. And you're each wedding planners?"

"Actually, no. Just me and Zaria even though Zaria is more of the visionary as far as flowers, decorating, and the overall ambience. I deal with the bridal party, the aspects of the ceremony, reception, and anything else to make sure everything runs smooth. Brooklyn is our accountant and photographer, and Addison plans other types of events like dinner parties, beach parties, and events for the younger crowd. We also have assistants and a few interns."

"That's great. I love to see young, independent women take charge of their own lives and start businesses of their own. It isn't always easy. Trust me, I've been there."

"No, it wasn't easy at all. Seems like you're doing well with your practice and now the concierge side of it."

"One of the best decisions I ever made. Another one was to change my morning routine and jog at the beach yesterday. Wouldn't have met you and we wouldn't be on our first ... outing."

Tossing the empty plastic bowl holding the waffle bowl into the garbage can a few yards in front of them, Reagan clapped when it landed in there. That rarely happened.

"You got skills, pretty lady. Let's see if I can do the same." He tossed his and it landed just on the edge of the can before falling in. "Yes!"

"The wind helped blow yours." Reagan started to giggle, but it turned into a yawn. Standing, she stretched and glanced at her watch. She noted the reluctant expression wash over his features as he stood and held out his arm to her. Wrapping hers around his, she snuggled close as she had a slight chill from the ice cream and the night breeze. "I guess we should call it an evening."

They walked in silence to the parking garage as her mind ran rampant of thoughts of kissing him good night.

Sliding her keys out of her dress pocket, Reagan pressed the button to unlock the trunk and handed him his tote bag. Shutting the trunk, she pivoted toward him and prayed she wouldn't give into the temptation to kiss him. "I had a lovely time. I look forward to hanging out with you on Sunday."

"Me too. I'll call you and we can discuss what we're going to do unless you already know of something else cool. You seem to enjoy creative things."

"I do. I'll let you know." Pausing, she sensed his thought process when he glanced at her mouth and he bit his bottom lip before settling seductive eyes on her with a questioning expression. Reagan needed to end the evening before she ended up in his arms and there would be no protesting from her. She stepped back. "Good night, Blake."

Reagan skirted out of his personal space and to the driver's side. Attempting to unlock the door, strong hands glided around her waist and turned her effortlessly to face him. Her heartbeat sped up like an Olympic sprinter who was in second place and wanted to bring the gold medal home for the team. He cocked his head to the side as he raised a curious eyebrow, and the gulp she tried to suppress emerged.

Can he hear the offbeat pace of my heart without a stethoscope?

"I don't get a hug good-bye?" he whispered, drawing her closer until she was engulfed in his embrace like a caterpillar in a cocoon.

His erotic scent filled the atmosphere, causing her heart to clench with anticipation of what she sensed was going to happen next. It was inevitable, especially when her lips parted on their own, betraying any thoughts of reminding herself that she wouldn't kiss him on the first date … well, outing. Wrapping her arms around his back, she stared up at him as a shiver prickled her skin. "Of course you can have a hug."

"And a kiss."

It was a statement not a question and while she didn't answer verbally, the heavy rise and fall of her breasts against his chest pretty much solidified it. The hardness and nearness of him scalded deep into her body. Though they weren't naked, she could feel his rigid, bare muscles on her skin. A rush of desire sprinted wildly through Reagan's veins when he gently brushed his lips on hers. Her eyes immediately shut as Blake yanked him to her even more, and she didn't think that was possible. Their bodies were already meshed together like magnets that couldn't be pried apart. The sensual kiss deepened as he stumbled them onto the driver door of the car. A moan of pleasure erupted during the slow wind of their tongues. It was a mixture of an unhurried yet fervent first kiss that she didn't want to end.

Intertwining his hands in her hair, Blake pushed more into her mouth as he sped up their zealous tryst. Another pleased moan released from her as she welcomed the warmth of his lips on hers. Reagan couldn't remember any of her first kisses being so in tuned before, but the connection transpiring between them was intensified with every passing second. He'd awakened a desire she'd suppressed over the years from always feeling the need to protect her heart. There was a different type of longing coasting through her body as he delved deeper into her mouth. It wasn't lustful or even seductive. It was a peaceful, relieved feeling that she couldn't explain.

She pulled back to catch her breath but more importantly to listen to the levelheaded good angel on her shoulder and not the bad one that kept whispering, "keep going, girl."

"Wow." Resting his hands on her hips, Blake kissed her forehead. "That was some kiss."

Her eyes fluttered shut again as his lips touched another part of her body, sending her mind to imagine all the ways he'd kiss every centimeter of her. "I was just thinking the same."

"Have you had your tongue registered yet?" he asked, winding his around hers again. "It's a lethal weapon, woman."A frustrated groan eased from his mouth as he kissed her lightly on the lips. "Mmm … damn, girl. Can't get enough of you. You taste like vanilla ice cream."

Shaking her head with a smirk, she touched his lips with her finger. "Probably for the same reason you taste like coffee ice cream."

"No, baby. It's definitely you."

"You're silly."

He drew her close once more, this time clenching her butt and imprisoning her lips in a hasty kiss that seemed to go on for hours. The burning sensations zipping through her body were erratic yet tantalizing. Ticklish vibrations landed in Reagan's center when he pressed even more on her and the feel of his erection against her caused a purr to escape her windpipes. The moans she made were unlike no sound she'd heard from herself before. In the distance, faint heels clicked on the pavement, a car alarm beeped, and a door slammed. Normally she'd care about public displays of affection, especially being pinned against a car about to fall over with ecstasy from a first kiss that had lasted longer than any other first kiss. However, being wrapped in Blake's strong embrace shut out the world like a protective shield around them.

"What are you doing to me?" he asked as a whisper on her lips.

"I should be asking you the same question considering I'd told myself I wasn't going to kiss you tonight." She paused and glanced around the parking garage that now had fewer cars than when they'd started their kiss. "And especially in a very public place like this."

"Glad you changed your mind."

The heat in his eyes burned with passion, and the temptation crashing over her didn't help with her trying to think wisely. She sensed he wanted to continue with their escapade, but she knew in her heart if they did she may do something she wouldn't regret. Reagan had to stop it now before she ended up in the backseat of her car like a naïve teenager on prom night.

"I should go," she whispered, relaxing her hold on him.

A cocky grin jerked up his jaw as he stepped back. "Okay. I know you don't want to because I don't either, but I agree. I can't rush anything with you. I enjoyed our evening, and I'd hate to mess up what could possibly be the best relationship either of us have ever had because we jumped too soon. Just know I'll be doing laps in my pool as soon as I arrive home. I'm not even going to turn on the pool heater. I need it ice cold."

She giggled. "I'll be in a cold shower, or I may need a skinny dip in the ocean."

"Great," he said through a gritted smile, opening the door for her. "Thanks for the visual."

"Oh, you're very welcome." She flung her purse on the passenger seat before plopping in hers. "I did have a lovely time. I look forward to our next outing."

"Me too. I'll think of something cool for us to do."

"Let me know."

"Text me when you make it home so I know you arrived safely."

"I will. Have a good night, Blake."

Bending down, he kissed her cheek. "I already did. Good night."

Once Reagan arrived home, she sent the text message as requested but didn't head straight to the cold shower or the ocean as she'd teased earlier. Blake's scent was tangled with hers, and she didn't want to erase it from her skin or clothes. Instead, she plopped on the couch, grabbed her late grandmother's quilt draped across the back, and snuggled inside of it. Closing her eyes, she transported back to being engulfed in his arms, and the warmth of his lips pierced hers once more. The fact that his cologne was still embedded on her dress sealed the lines of reality and fantasy.

Reagan couldn't remember the last time she'd felt secure and carefree enough to be swept up in a man's arms like that. She'd had her share of first kisses, but they didn't leave her in a state of pure pleasure arousal. And the arousal wasn't sexual. If that was the case she would've indeed invited him back to her place. No, it was an uncanny feeling that she couldn't explain. However, for the first time in a long while, she was anxious for a second date. The smile plastered on her face changed into a giggle as she wrapped the quilt tighter around her. Her eyes opened and landed on the colorful masterpiece that had her grandmother's and other female family member's wedding gowns and other family mementos. Material from Justin's son's baby blanket and Zaria's wedding gown were the last to be sewn on at the bottom. It was the last time her grandmother had added to the quilt before she died six months after her husband, and now Reagan was responsible for continuing the tradition of the Richardson family quilt.

Her memory flashed back to Zaria and Garrett's wedding day, over a year ago, when Zaria tossed her bridal bouquet purposely in Reagan's direction. It landed at her feet and she almost didn't pick it up because marriage was nowhere on her to-do list. Plan weddings for others? Yes. Plan her own wedding? No. She wasn't like most women who dreamed of their special day since they were little girls and even went as far as to have a book loaded with ideas. Reagan hadn't an inkling of what she wanted and couldn't even imagine her wedding day. She'd planned classy and elegant events on a budget to elaborate, over-the-top sophisticated affairs, but for some reason she couldn't envision her own. It seemed to be an unattainable fantasy that would never happen.

However, tonight something changed and the thought of starting a book actually crept into her thoughts. It was a small detail but she knew she wanted it. Ice cream. She laughed at the silly, out-of-nowhere idea. Though as she drifted off to sleep an hour later, Reagan could faintly taste the coffee ice cream on her lips and made a mental note to jot down her absurd thought in a wedding book. *Her wedding book.*

Chapter Four

"Love this idea you had," Brooklyn commented to Reagan as they set up their folding Adirondack chairs on the light brown sand at the beach behind Reagan's home. "After dealing with bridezilla today, I could use a little beach relaxation."

"I'm sure she's just nervous. We see it all the time."

Brooklyn let out a chuckle. "True, but it was still a long day. However, in the end she was very grateful and pleased with the pictures. She sort of reminded me of you. I can only imagine how our lives will be when planning the ultimate wedding for the wedding planner who leaves no stone unturned."

Reagan laughed sarcastically even though Brooklyn was sort of correct. After the revelation of actually thinking about her own wedding, Reagan knew it had to be perfect but most importantly the groom had to be the one or the wedding wouldn't matter years down the road if she was in an unhappy, loveless marriage.

Pulling an oversized floppy pink and orange sun hat from her tote bag, Reagan placed it over her hair and plopped into the chair. Kicking off her pink flip flops, she curled her feet under her, sighed deep, and closed her eyes to soak in the warmth of the sun. One of the main reasons for moving to St. Simons Island was the warm weather the majority of the time year unlike Memphis and Atlanta. Now her favorite pastime was relaxing on the beach with the rays beaming on her while reading or staring out to the sea. It was rare to have a free afternoon, for her work days usually ended after five so the times she could escape to the beach for an hour were welcomed. Though she usually preferred her alone time, she invited Brooklyn today who had returned to the office frustrated after an engagement photo shoot around the island.

Handing Reagan her iPad that displayed the pictures, Brooklyn settled in her chair, pulled her shoulder-length brown hair into a ponytail, and rubbed sunscreen on her bare arms and legs. The ladies shook their heads and smiled as they noticed they wore the same pink bikini with black piping. The best friends had a habit of dressing alike without consulting with each other.

Reagan swiped through the pictures. "These turned out beautiful. I think the one with them by the lighthouse staring at each other lovingly should be the one for their engagement announcement cards."

She continued to peruse the pictures and was impressed with Brooklyn's keen eye for detail. They'd been best friends, more like sisters, since elementary school along with their big brothers, Justin and Rasheed, who were also best friends. She'd witnessed Brooklyn take an interest in photography at a young age and had turned the hobby into a part time career while obtaining her MBA. When Reagan had first dreamed of owning her own event planning company, she knew Brooklyn would be the perfect fit along with Zaria.

"I agree, but I also like the one of them lying on the grass with his hand stroking her hair. I think we'll enlarge this one for the engagement party." Reagan paused as Brooklyn pulled a thermos out of her mini ice cooler and two red plastic cups. "I'm going to assume that isn't hot chocolate," she teased, taking one of the cups as Brooklyn poured the drink into it.

"Georgia peach margaritas."

"Even better." Sipping her drink, Reagan nodded her head and took another sip. "You know if we're ever short a bartender you could definitely help out. This drink is delish."

"Thanks, girl, but then who would take pictures?" Brooklyn teased.

Reagan giggled at her blonde moment. "Oh yeah. So how are you enjoying having Addison camped out in her tiny home in your backyard?"

"First of all, I still can't believe she actually had a tiny house built. I told her she could stay in my guestroom for as long as she needed."

"She probably wanted her own space. Plus, she likes to hike and travel. All she has to do is hitch it up to her Ford 150 truck and be on her way."

"Yeah, I guess it's the new, hip thing for her age group. At twenty-five I was living in a studio apartment above your brother's blues club and hanging out on Beale Street all the time. Now at thirty-two I couldn't imagine doing that. I'm usually asleep by ten o'clock on most nights if we're not working."

"I hear you." Reagan sipped her drink and contemplated bringing up the next subject. "She mentioned Chase will be in town soon to visit her."

At the mention of Chase Arrington, Brooklyn glared at Reagan momentarily before taking a gulp of her drink. "Stop."

"What?" she asked as innocently as possible. "I'm not the one who has a huge photo blown up of Addison's big brother on my wall."

Brooklyn's forehead wrinkles emerged in an aggravated stance. "There's hundreds of pictures on the wall."

"But his is in the middle, the biggest, and the immediate focal point. Brook, I don't blame you. Chase and his twin brother Hunter are very handsome men. Even though the one of Hunter with his wife is barely noticeable. It's just lost in the crowd with the rest but your boo is smack dab in the middle."

"Whatever. I just like the angle and the lighting of the picture. He seems deep in thought, and … well, I don't know. There's something about it that's intriguing. Its art."

"True. Plus, being suave and debonair in a tuxedo with the bow tie hanging off, top two buttons loose, and a drink in his hand had nothing to do with it. Or his smooth, chocolate skin, bald head, and his glasses that make him appear like an irresistible nerd … which has always been your type."

"He's not a nerd," Brooklyn said in a defensive tone. "He's just highly intelligent."

"And how would you know? You've barely spoken two words to the man in almost eight years since you met him at Justin and Shelbi's wedding. I've witnessed him try to hold conversations with you, but you've always found some excuse to walk away."

"I've only seen him at a few weddings over the years. I'm working. I don't have time to chit chat."

Reagan's lips swished to the side at Brooklyn's attempt to steer away from the fact that she had a crush on Chase. "If you say so."

The beep of Reagan's cell phone from her tote bag startled them both, and Brooklyn's sigh of relief signaled she was glad for the interruption. Retrieving the phone, Reagan couldn't contain a smile upon seeing a text from Blake. It had been two days since their outing and their provocative first kiss that still burned her lips upon reminiscing about it. They hadn't seen each other, but they'd been having a pleasant time of texting and chatting. She was ready for Sunday to hurry the hell up. And apparently, he couldn't wait either.

Is it Sunday yet?

She couldn't help but smile at his question. *Four more days.*

Since you like different types of outings, one of my patients is a dance instructor and has offered to give us private salsa lessons.

That sounds like fun.

Do you know how to salsa?

Nope.

Cool. I'll set it up for Sunday. Until then, sweetheart.

"Well, damn. Who has you all hot and bothered?"

Reagan turned to see Brooklyn staring over the top of her shades, and a sly smirk slid across her sienna face. Taking a sip of her drink, Reagan tried to suppress a smile but it was no use as the heat rushed to her cheeks, followed by a giggle that burst through. "It was Blake."

"Wow. One date and you've been on a high ever since. You're not usually this giddy over a guy."

"Giddy? You make it sound like I'm a lovesick teenager." *Even though I kinda do feel that way.* "And it wasn't a date. It was an out—"

"Yeah. Yeah. Outing. Smouting. Call it what you want, but no one beams like that over an outing or kiss on a non-date. Heck, yesterday you practically burned the shrimp while humming a love song."

Okay, fine I burned the shrimp, but I'm not going to admit to it.

"No, I was cooking *Cajun* shrimp and grits and the song was Pachelbel's 'Canon in D'. You know it's always stuck in my head. It's a wedding song," Reagan teased, but the funny disdain on Brooklyn's face screamed that Reagan was lying. "Okay. Fine. I had a lovely time and I can't wait until I see him again. He's a nice guy. At least *I* can admit when I like someone," she teased, pinching her best friend's arm.

Brooklyn smacked her lips and pinched Reagan's upper arm back. "Anyway, this isn't about me. Zaria has been telling you about Blake for over a year and you never wanted to meet him, but I guess fate intervened."

"I was in a relationship at the time."

"With someone you didn't even like," Brooklyn reminded. "You dumped him and the other one afterward so fast I barely knew either them. In fact, you've broken up with every boyfriend you've ever had since we were in high school. And you've only had five real boyfriends, uh well … if you want to call them that for they never last long. Everyone else was just a few dates and then you stop taking their calls. Zaria and I had a bet going on how long the last one would last. Needless to say, I won. I told her four months tops but she swore a year since he was practically in love with you. I swear as soon as they say the L word or have any inkling that they want forever you sprint faster than a cheetah."

"I'm not that bad … am I?" Reagan questioned Brooklyn but she was really questioning herself. She knew all of what her friend stated was true, but she wasn't that into any of them. She hadn't found her Prince Charming or her Mr. Right, more like Mr. Right Now, and that's not what she wanted. Unlike her mother, she wasn't going to settle only to be heartbroken twice over by the same man. While her mother, Lillian, had only been in her life for barely four years, Reagan knew everything about her thanks to Justin and their grandparents. She suspected her mother wouldn't want her to endure the same hardships and mistakes. Her grandmother instilled in her to never settle for any man or their BS, and Reagan made up her mind a long time ago that she wasn't going to. Her grandparents had a loving marriage for over fifty years and she wanted the same.

"I think with what's-his-face that was a teacher I just wanted to be in relationship for the sake of saying I had a man because at the time everyone I knew had a boyfriend or were at least dating."

"You were on the rebound from the other what's-his-face before him. Still, can't believe he lasted almost a year."

"Well, I left him in and his trifling ass in Atlanta. When I found out he had a son that he didn't acknowledge and wasn't even paying child support that was the deal breaker."

"Sooooo, there must be another outing with Blake because you were definitely cheesing over that text."

"Yep. Salsa dance lessons on Sunday."

"Mmm … romantic and different."

"Exactly. Who wants to do the same type of boring dinner and a movie dates. You learn more about a person with creative types of interactions."

"Really? And when did you realize this newfound way of dating?"

"Zaria suggested I have fun and get to know him and just be me. I want to try something new this go around."

"Keep me posted. Perhaps, I need to try this too even though my dating life is nonexistent at the moment."

"Or maybeeeeeee, he'll be here soon to visit his sister," Reagan said in a sing-song voice, referring to Chase Arrington once more. "You can take pictures of him without his knowledge for your wall collage. Or your private collection."

Brooklyn laughed nonchalantly and poured another margarita.

*****

The urgent ring of the cell phone awoke Reagan out of her peaceful, deep sleep. She'd drifted off as soon as her head had hit the pillow at midnight after a long day with two weddings and one reception. Frowning as she glanced at the time on the antique Benjamin Banneker clock on the glass nightstand, she became concerned as to why Justin would call so early on a Sunday morning. It was barely 8:00 a.m. and he was aware she usually slept until noon on her only day off unless she had an event.

"Hey, big brother," she answered the phone in a groggy state.

"Didn't mean to wake you, but I wanted to give you a heads up about something."

"What's up?" she asked, yawning.

"Our father stopped by the restaurant last night."

"So he really did keep his promise this time. Shocking. I assume he wanted something and it must be important. Money? A kidney? A lung?" she asked sarcastically. "Blood?"

"Close."

"Huh?" Sitting up against the pillows, she was wide awake now. "What do you mean close? Don't tell me he really does want your kidney?"

"Not an organ, but he needs a bone marrow transplant."

Her hand flew to her mouth as she gasped out loud. "Why?"

"He has myelodysplastic syndrome. It's a form of cancer."

"I've never heard of it."

"Robin Roberts from *Good Morning America* had it after having had breast cancer some years before. Her sister was the donor."

"Oh, yeah. I do remember that. So he's asked you for bone marrow?"

"Yep, or at least do a test to see if mine is a match as opposed to going through the bone marrow registry, but I haven't decided what to do. I've been numb all night. He also asked if I thought you would see if you're a match just in case."

"Me? I barely know that man. Heck, you barely know him, but now all of a sudden he needs his children's help? Was he there when we needed him? Was he there when you broke your leg or when I had to be hospitalized when I had the chicken pox? Did he attend our graduations and birthday parties? Was he at your wedding even though you invited him? No, to all of my questions, yet he needs our bone marrow. And yet after all that, I'm scared for him, Justin. What should we do?"

"Reagan, I know we aren't close with him, but I am going to give it some thought. My conscious won't let me just completely shut him out. I do understand how you feel. That was pretty much my initial reaction."

"You seem to be considering this."

"I don't know. I guess my shock has slightly worn off and I'm curious to know if I'm a match."

"What does Shelbi think?"

"She says whatever I decide she'll support my decision. From a medical standpoint, the doctor in her feels the registry should be the last resort if a family member such as a sibling or child is a match and is physically able to do it."

"Doesn't he have a brother? Wouldn't that be a higher match?"

"He died a few years ago. It's just us."

Flinging off her satin bonnet, she swiped her hand in her hair and prayed that she was still asleep and having the worst nightmare ever. "How soon do we have to do the test?"

"Within the next few weeks. So you're considering it?"

"I don't know," she replied quietly. "I need to time to process this."

"I understand. He asked for your new number, by the way, but I figured you'd kill me if I gave it to him so I'll text his to you if you care to speak to him."

Throwing the comforter back, she swung her legs out of the bed and trekked across her bedroom and out into the hallway toward the kitchen. She needed coffee stat even though a shot of whiskey would've been more appropriate to calm down her rising anxiety. "Slow down, Justin. I'm not there yet."

"No problem. I understand. Just think about it and do some research."

"Okay."

"I gotta go head back to the kitchen. Jazz brunch starts in a few hours."

"Mmm ... wish I was in Memphis," she said, filling the carafe with water and deciding what to eat for breakfast now that she was wide awake. "I love your jazz brunches. Will your blueberry and walnut waffles be on the menu along with your famous barbeque beef stuffed biscuits? Oh, and your shrimp and grits."

"Of course. All of my patrons' favorites."

"I need to hop on a plane right now." She hadn't been home to Memphis since Christmas and homesickness always sunk in when chatting with Justin.

"I wish you could hop on a plane, baby sis. We miss you. I can't hug you through the phone."

"I miss you guys, too. I guess if one of us goes through with the bone marrow transplant I'll be home either way. However, I don't want to think about it right now, but if you're a match and you decide to do it, of course I'll be there for you."

"Thanks, Reagan. I appreciate it."

"Go cook, Chef Richardson, and try not to let this consume you or burn any food."

"Now you know I don't burn food."

"I know. Love you, big bro. Talk to you later."

After hanging up, Reagan waited impatiently for her coffee to brew while she cooked a veggie omelet stuffed with broccoli, spinach, peppers, and oozing with Swiss cheese. She tried to block the information her brother had presented to her, yet she couldn't help but think about it. Their father had barely made time for them in his life and now he expected them to come to his rescue. Today was supposed to be a fun-filled day learning how to salsa dance with Blake and getting to know him better. Instead, the thought of making a possible life or death decision would surely cloud her mind. Reagan never handled stress well, which was why she'd signed up for yoga classes, kickboxing lessons, meditation courses, and swim aerobics over the years to relieve stress. Her mother's heart condition had always bothered Reagan, and even though her blood pressure and cholesterol levels were fine, she always made an effort to eat healthy, stay active, and live a simple, drama-free life as much as possible.

Happy to hear the beep of the coffee maker, Reagan grabbed an extra large travel mug from the cabinet and filled it with the piping hot liquid that tickled her nose with the extra robust aroma. Taking a calming sip, her mind escaped to the long day ahead with salsa followed by dinner. She didn't know what restaurant, but Blake had promised she would love the cuisine and the chef was a friend of his who would make sure they were satisfied.

Reflecting on her father's illness spilled into her thoughts for the rest of the morning while she tried on various dresses, including three that Zaria dropped off and demanded as sweet as possible that she wear one of the sexy frocks. After deciding on one of her cousin's suggestions and texting a picture for approval, Reagan jumped in the shower and prayed that today's outing with Blake would distract her from crying. Despite her rant earlier, she truly did love her father and deep down had always wanted to be a daddy's girl.

Chapter Five

"Stunning," Blake complimented Reagan, scanning a quick eye over her as she sashayed into the lobby of the dance studio. He had to force himself not to salivate over the light blue, straight dress hugging her dangerous curvy hips. The sexy V dip of the neckline rested between her small yet perky mounds that jiggled every time her heels touched the hardwood floor, causing a gulp to stick in his throat. A slit up the side of her right thigh was tasteful enough to be not too provocative yet left his imagination in shambles of provocative ideas. Yanking up the hem came to mind, and the knowing curve of her mouth hinted she read his thoughts.

The woman was sexy without trying. To wear a dress like that for their salsa lesson was sure to have him thinking about puppies and kittens just so the tug that pulled at his briefs when she'd entered would settle down. Otherwise he wouldn't be able to dance and would end up either stepping on her strappy black heels or finding the nearest private place to kiss her. Even though after their first kiss, apparently neither of them cared about whether or not privacy was an issue. He had never been one for public displays of affection, but Reagan had awakened a passion in him that didn't care about where they were as long as her lips were on his.

"Thank you." Approaching, Reagan smiled pleasantly as she ran a gaze over his dark blue dress shirt and black slacks. "I hope I'm not too late. Spring break has started and it was hell crossing the bridge."

Blake barely heard what she said after "thank you" for he was drawn to her succulent lips that he'd had the pleasure to kiss and distracted his thoughts since the last time he'd tasted them.

Clearing his throat, Blake held out his hand and led her inside of the dance studio. He smiled as he saw their reflections throughout the large room whose three of the four walls were mirrors. He cursed himself for not kissing her in the lobby as Maria Gomez, the dance instructor, approached holding out her arms for a hug from Reagan. Maria was friendly toward everyone and had been nagging him like his mother to date, but this was definitely over the top.

"Reagan, darling," Maria said, as the women hugged. "What a pleasant surprise."

"Oh wow! I had no idea you were today's instructor. You're usually off on Sundays."

"Yes, but it was a special request from my favorite doctor." Maria let go of Reagan and patted Blake's cheek. "He said he had a hermosa amiga he wanted to impress on a special kind of date. He takes good care of me and my husband. I couldn't refuse. Had no idea it was you, though."

"And I didn't think you were the instructor considering this isn't your studio."

"Si, senorita. My studio is being used today for ballroom dance sessions in all the rooms, so Dr. Harrison rented this one for us to use this afternoon," the older lady said, twisting her jet-black hair streaked with a few grays into a bun on the top of her head.

Blake's forehead indented. "Small world. You've had dance lessons with Senora Gomez before?" he asked, worried that this wouldn't be a one-of-a-kind outing for her.

"No. I refer my clients to her. Some of my couples want to learn the waltz or just need to learn basic two-step dancing for their wedding dance."

Relieved, Blake nodded. "Ah, yes. That makes perfect sense. Has anyone requested the salsa? That would be cool for a first dance, or a second I suppose. First dances are usually slow dancing, right?" he asked Reagan.

"Mmm … no one has done the salsa but believe it or not with these modern day brides and grooms, I've seen all types of the first dance. Every bride and groom's favorite song isn't always a slow one, and I encourage them to add their own personality and flair in every aspect of their special day. I had one couple that started out slow dancing and then switched it up and did the winning routine from the movie *Dirty Dancing*. Couples are being quite creative these days. No more slow dancing to their favorite love song."

Maria chimed in, "Oh, and don't forget the bride who had me choreograph the entire wedding party to the routine from Michael Jackson's 'Remember the Time' video."

"That was the best," Reagan said with a beaming, bright smile. "The guests were literally trying to join in at the end. It was an amazing night."

Blake glanced at Reagan as her face lit up. It was on the tip of his tongue to ask her what she wanted their first wedding dance to be. Wrinkling his brow, he wondered why on earth had that thought even popped into his head. It was only their second date yet he could see himself married to a woman like Reagan, if not her. His heart contracted when the idea of it not being her entered his psyche. A voice inside of him shouted at the top of its lungs, "Hell no, it has to be her." *Only her.*

Clearing his throat and his crazy mind for pondering the future with a woman he'd just met, he placed his focus back on the ladies as Maria announced she was ready to begin their lesson.

Forty-five minutes later, they'd learned the basic steps of the salsa including a right turn and had managed to stop counting out loud. He'd thought of the salsa as a sexy yet fun dance; however, learning it was more technical than he'd realized. So far they'd stumbled over each other, stepped on each other's shoes, and laughed louder than he could remember on any date.

Maria turned off the music and clapped. "Okay, you two. Great job, but now I want you to stop glancing down at your feet and look at each other. Stare into each other's eyes and trust that you and your partner's feet are doing the steps the correctly. Just trust each other and communicate with your eyes and moves. Let it flow through you sensually, as if you're one."

"Oh, boy." Reagan swiped her hands through her hair. "Okay, we can do this and I'll try hard not to step on your feet ... again."

Her expression was bashful yet cute and he couldn't help but to think how adorable she was even in the sexy dress that had his mind racing with wicked thoughts ever since she strolled in.

"That's okay. You can just massage them later," he teased.

Shaking her head in the negative, Reagan swished her mouth to the side. "That's not going to happen."

"I'd massage yours ... and any other body part that may need my attention."

For a moment, he'd forgotten they weren't alone as Reagan's eyes widened in huge circles and an embarrassed smile emerged from both of them as Maria laughed.

"You two are a mess, and I love it," Maria said, patting their cheeks and walking back to the CD player. "Let's begin again and remember what I said."

Blake took his left hand and picked up Reagan's right hand and placed his right hand on her upper back as she rested her left hand on his right shoulder. Maria turned the music back on and Reagan moved backwards first as they'd practiced when he pushed on her right hand for the three steps back and then slightly pulled with his other hand to move her toward him for three steps forward. As they continued, Maria encouraged them to have fun and not worry about mistakes.

"Ahh … muy bien," Maria complimented. "You were marvelous. Now practice your turns. I'll be right back," she said, pivoting and vanishing through a side door.

As they turned, Reagan stumbled on her four-inch heels and fell over. He snatched her to him before she hit the floor. He held her close to him, almost in a protective cocoon, and the thought of always wanting to keep her safe even from something as simple as a fall filled his head. *What is this woman doing to me?*

Pushing her hair out of her face, he gave a reassuring smile while cupping her chin. "Hi there." Blake gripped Reagan around the waist with one arm. "I have you."

"Thank you." Resting her palms on his chest, she exhaled for a moment. "That was embarrassing."

"No worries. You aren't going to fall … well, maybe for me." A sly grin rose up the left side of his face and the temptation to touch her trembling lips in an erotic kiss drove him crazy.

"Mmm … oh really?" she asked, trying to purse a smirk. "You got it like that, Doc?"

"Most definitely." He ran a finger along her neck, causing her pouty lips to part into a sensual moan that stirred deep into his stomach. "See? You just made my point and I haven't even kissed you the way I really wanted to. I was just being a gentleman the other night."

"Whatever." She rolled her eyes away from him and encircled his neck with her hands. "Perhaps you're falling for me considering you couldn't get enough of me the other evening."

"That makes two of us."

A beep from her purse on the bench by the door sent both their eyes to it.

"You need to answer it?" he asked. He really hated that whoever the hell it was had interrupted him from snatching her to him and kissing her before Maria returned.

"Unfortunately, yes," she said, breaking their embrace and heading toward her purse. "I'm expecting a call about a last-minute wedding cake change." Sliding the cell phone out of a side pocket, her beautiful face scrunched into horror as she read the message. Shaking her head, she tossed the phone back into her purse but didn't move.

He jetted to her at once as concernment built up in his chest. Whatever changed her mood from ecstatic and upbeat to upset and almost in tears, he needed to punch it.

"What's wrong? That was clearly not about cake."

She placed her hand on her forehead and inhaled, trying to display a smile that ended up in a crooked frown. "No, but its … uh … nothing." She took his hand, squeezing it hard, and led him back to the middle of the dance floor. "Let's continue. We have twenty minutes left of our salsa session."

He halted them in place, ignoring the fact that Maria re-entered the room. "No, what's wrong?"

"I'm fine. Really. Just a surprise text message reminding me of something that I hadn't thought about since I arrived. That's all."

"Some ex-boyfriend I need to have a little talk with for upsetting my lady?" he asked seriously. He noted a tiny gleam in her eyes when he said "my lady."

"No. Calm down." She patted his chest. "Nothing like that."

He figured she'd have no reason to lie to him. "Mmkay. We'll finish," he commented reluctantly, taking the salsa form with her once more. "But if you need to talk or vent, I'm here. Or if I need to have a man-to-man discussion with some punk, let me know."

"That won't be necessary at all, but thank you."

They continued with Maria giving them a few pointers but the dismal and far away expression on Reagan's face over the text message placed a damper over their date. He hated that something was amiss yet he understood if she didn't want to confide in him considering they'd just met. However, he wanted … no, needed to know her on all levels and the fact that she wasn't happy made him feel even more protective of her.

Once they said their good-byes to Maria, he slid Reagan's hand into his and walked her outside to her car.

"That was awesome. Thank you, Blake," she said sincerely, squeezing his hand. "I really needed that."

"I'm glad you enjoyed it."

Sighing, she stared up at him with wistful eyes and his heart nearly cracked. "Are you going to tell me now?"

"You're so thoughtful and concerned but really it's nothing. Just some family stuff." She tilted her head and tapped her chin. "Mmm … maybe you could give me some medical advice, though."

"Of course." He was somewhat relieved it wasn't an ex bothering or stalking her. However, now he hoped that whatever the medical issue with the family member wasn't too serious. Every time her face saddened it literally punctured a hole in his heart.

"Cool." Fishing around in her purse, she pulled out the keys to her Mercedes. "I'll follow you to the restaurant, and we'll discuss it over dinner."

"You can ride with me. You know men usually pick women up for dates."

"True … but maybe I don't want you to know where I live." Winking, she opened her car door. "I'll follow. Where are we going?"

"My houseboat."

She eyed him carefully, crossing her arms across her chest. "I've never heard of that restaurant."

"No … I mean *my* houseboat. I own one. I tend to stay there on the weekends, and before you think I'm trying to lure you into my bed, my fishing buddy who is a chef is there preparing our dinner." And while he meant what he said, he couldn't help but think of her naked in his bed with all of her limbs intertwined and twisted with his.

"Mmm-hmm."

"Trust me, I may have some indecent thoughts in my head, but I'm trying my damnedest to stick to getting to know you better. Though after that first kiss, its hard as hell." *Literally. No pun intended.*

"Then perhaps we shouldn't kiss anymore."

"Wait a minute, woman—" Blake started to protest, but she grabbed him to her and kissed him lightly on the lips. Wrapping her in his embrace, he drove his tongue deeper between her lips to convince her otherwise.

"Calm down," she said in a whisper, kissing him once again. "I was joking with you."

"That has to be the most unfunniest joke I've ever heard. You could never be on *Def Comedy Jam*."

"Well, you're really going to hate my four-month rule." Releasing him, she slid into her car and shut the door.

"Four-month rule?" He was almost scared to ask even though he knew what she was referring to. However, he wasn't surprised nor was it a turn off. Sex with Reagan, while it had crossed his mind, wasn't the reason he wanted to date her. He'd lusted after women and had sex way too early in relationships that apparently didn't last considering he was single. Reagan stirred something deeper in him than any woman he'd ever met and waiting wouldn't be the end of the world. Sure, he'd have to add in a few extra laps a week in his pool or dive off the side of his houseboat directly into the ocean. Though he had an inkling they would never have sex because if the

59

connection they shared continued to grow, making love would be the only course of action.

Chapter Six

"This is not a houseboat." Shaking her head in the negative, Reagan pivoted toward Blake as they stood on the boardwalk leading to a white, two-story, modern houseboat ... or rather yacht in her opinion. It sat among a row of true houseboats that were smaller and not as grand. Attached to it was a small speed boat with the name Lola printed in calligraphy. On the top deck, there was a middle-aged woman setting a table. She waved to them before disappearing inside.

"This is a small *yacht*," she stated, matter-of-factly.

He remained quiet as a bashful smirk painted his face. Blake intertwined his hand in hers as they continued along the marina where the boat was docked.

"Who's Lola?"

"My mother."

"Does your houseboat have a name as well?" The area under the first floor lounge deck where she assumed a boat's name would be placed was empty, but she figured it could be on the other side hidden from her view.

"No. Not yet. My mother suggested I name it after my wife, but ..." He shrugged, stopping the sentence.

Wife? Somewhat taken aback, her heart *raced* and a feeling of nausea over swept her until he started to laugh.

"Calm down. She means *when* I'm married. Don't worry. I'm single."

"Oh, yes. Of course. Just making sure." A sigh of relief escaped Reagan's throat as she thought back to a date a few years ago with a man who'd neglected to tell her until the third date he was married but allegedly separated with two children. She jumped up from the dinner table, called a taxi, and never saw him again. Ever since then she preferred to meet at the designated place considering it wasn't the first time she'd left in the middle of a date without her car.

"Do you take it out for a spin?" she asked, picturing him behind a huge wheel, navigating it and wearing a captain's hat with little else for some reason. *Why do I keep trying to imagine this man naked?*

"Yep. My dad taught me and my sisters when we were teenagers. When our family comes together for water sports, we take this boat out for my mom to relax and the motor boat for water skiing, parasailing, and such with my sisters and their families. My dad owns the boat I use for deep sea fishing, and he has an actual yacht called The Lola. In another lifetime, I swear we were all fish. Do you like water sports?"

"Most definitely. I enjoy water skiing but I really love jet skiing."

"Cool. If I'd known I would've brought mine today. I keep them locked in my garage."

"How about next time," she suggested. Reagan couldn't remember the last time words flowed freely from her lips, but she wanted a next time with him again and again. It was like seeing her future flash before her eyes whenever either of them mentioned seeing the other again. It was almost like a duh moment, as if what else could they possibly be doing if they weren't doing it together. She knew it sounded silly thinking it, but as a hopeless romantic—for her clients yet never for herself—she sort of imagined what all of her blushing brides were experiencing when they would go on and on about what a wonderful and loving man they were marrying.

Blake halted, turned her toward him, and kissed her forehead with the most tender and enduring kiss, sending a swift shiver to run through her body. She hated how this man was breaking down her defenses but at the same time loved every moment of it. Earlier, when she'd blurted out her four-month rule, it was more so of a reminder to herself and not a warning to him. The way he was being protective and concerned about the text message she received from her father had caused her vulnerability to rise. She couldn't give into temptation despite the fact she'd spent a majority of their salsa lesson fantasizing about the horizontal tango. She usually reserved those thoughts for celebrity men she had the hots for, not a man she was only on date number two with. The way he held her close to him and took the lead during the dance, awakened a desire deep in her for Blake to take the lead in other ways and guide them on a dance that only they knew the sensual, seductive steps to.

"Mmm … what was that for?" she asked, gazing up at his eyes, which had deepened to a seductive midnight black even though his natural eye color was dark brown. Her memories skated back to a time when Zaria stated that when a man's eyes darkened, that meant he's turned on. Of course Reagan, who was in middle school at the time, didn't believe it. However, Zaria claimed to know more about men thanks to being one month older and because she would sneak to read her mother's racy romance novels. Afterwards, she'd share all the sexy parts with Brooklyn and Reagan.

However, now that Blake's eyes were indeed almost midnight black, she hoped that there was some truth in Zaria's theory.

"Love the way you see us together in the future." A half-smile settled on his lips and his voice lowered. "I do, too. It's almost scary, woman, yet I can't wait to see what the future holds for us."

"I totally agree." Reagan slid from his embrace before she forfeited the four-month rule.

"Ready to go aboard?" He held out his arm as she slid hers around it. "My mother's assistant, Kara, has everything set up for us on the top deck."

"Yes, and I smell something rather delicious."

Walking up the ramp, he slid open one of the floor-to-ceiling, tinted glass doors and motioned for her to enter. "That would be the speckled trout and shrimp I caught yesterday along with cheese grits and my mother's recipe for homemade biscuits."

"Sounds wonderful. I love fresh seafood. One of the perks of living here. Do you cook?" she asked as they entered a gorgeous living area with plush white leather couches that lined either side of the wall of windows. To her left she could see the mini-gourmet kitchen through the opened double French doors. The antique white cabinets, stainless steel appliances, and the huge island in the center were more elaborate than her kitchen at home. She'd bought an older fixer upper when she moved to the island, and while she'd started on renovations, her kitchen was the last project on the list. The Precious Moments side of the house took precedence over her living quarters.

"Nah. I'm more of a fish fry and barbeque man." After offering to take her purse, he set it on a nearby credenza with family pictures on it. "I make a mean angus burger stuffed with bleu cheese and topped with fried shrimp. My version of surf and turf."

"That's different. We'll have to cook one day." For a moment, she imagined herself in Blake's houseboat kitchen making breakfast with him and had to shake it from her thoughts before that suggestion poured from her lips.

"I'd like that. Nothing better than a home-cooked meal."

Blake turned toward the chef as he approached them, wiping his hands on a dish towel. His salt and pepper hair was tied back in a ponytail at the nape of his neck, and he wore a Atlanta Falcon's shirt. "Hey, Walter. Dinner smells wonderful."

"Thank you, and you're just in time. The stuffed trout just came out of the oven."

They followed him into the kitchen where all of the food was laid out on the island causing Reagan's stomach to rumble with delight, and she hoped the gentlemen didn't hear. After her conversation with Justin that morning, she'd barely touched her breakfast, but now she was starved. And even though she hadn't told Blake what was bothering her yet, she felt a tad better knowing that he was genuinely concerned about her feelings.

"Walt, this is Reagan Richardson."

Walter nodded his head in approval and glanced at Blake with amused blue eyes. "You're even lovelier than Blake said. Now I see why he has me over here on my only day off."

"Well, thank you, and its very nice to meet you."

"Blake tells me you're a chef as well?"

"No, no. Not really." She waved her hands in front of her. "My brother is the chef. He owns a blues restaurant back home in Memphis. It's more of a hobby for me."

"That's how it started with me, and now I'm catering everyone's private parties. I hope you enjoy dinner."

"I'm sure I will. Everything looks and smells delish."

Walter turned toward Blake. "Well, I gotta get going. Kara will be here for a little while longer if you need anything."

Blake patted Walter on the back, walking him out into the living area. "I appreciate it, man. Tell the Mrs. I said hello."

After the chef left, Kara appeared and suggested they go to the top deck and she'd bring everything up there.

Reagan followed Blake to a hallway leading to a set of spiral stairs and a second floor landing. She glanced down the hallway laden with closed doors before they headed out a door onto the deck. She couldn't help but wonder if his bedroom was behind one of the closed doors and shook her head free of the image of being intertwined with Blake in his bed.

"Wow. It's breathtaking up here." Reagan admired the scene before her as she could see the water go on for miles and miles. A cool spring breeze blew a calming chill over her. "I see why you come every weekend. I think I'd be here in this very spot every day and night."

When Blake encircled her waist from behind, it perked up her sense of touch and she let the sensual wave of promise cascade over her. Resting his chin on her shoulder, he drew her all the way against his body, which engulfed her in a feeling of being shielded from all harm.

"I'll keep that in mind." He kissed the side of her neck, causing an amorous moan to release from her.

His whisper was deep and seductive, seeming more of a promise of what would eventually transpire between them. Reagan shuddered with anticipation, plus his lips on her neck didn't help either. She already knew from their first kiss that he could be gentle and aggressive all at the same time, so placing kisses on other parts or hopefully every inch of her skin, was sure to be exquisite. The thought was intoxicating, and she hadn't even had a sip of the white wine she'd spotted on the table.

Perhaps I should just stick to the water before I find myself jumping over board to cool off.

He led her to a chair as Kara placed their plates full of the delectable food on the candle lit table. The sun had just begun to set and it shimmered on the ocean in bright hues of yellow and orange. Once they were alone, he poured the wine followed by blessing the food. They ate in silence for the most part except for her sharing with him the weddings from yesterday and compliments for the chef over how wonderful the food was.

"I'm going to have to jog the beach twice in the morning," he said, before taking another bite of his shrimp and grits.

"I may have to skip yoga and pop in one of my Shaun T Beach Body work out DVDs. Everything is …" She paused as an adorable frown slid over his face. "What?"

"If you don't go to yoga, what do I have to look forward to in the morning?"

"You're sweet, but next time tell Chef Walter to make me a salad!" she teased, sipping her wine. "Just kidding. Thank you for today. You really got my mind off of something I don't want to think about."

"You're welcome, pretty lady. That's what I'm here for."

The statement softened his features into a sincere understanding that there was an issue bothering her and the genuineness in his voice touched her deeply. Blake's compassionate stare sunk into her soul, and at that moment she was struck with the epiphany that she could share anything with him.

Taking a sip of her wine, she breathed deep. "My estranged father sent me a text," she blurted out.

Shock rested in his eyes as his fork filled with trout stayed raised mid-air. "Oh. When was the last time you saw him?"

"Right before I moved here. So three years, but I've spoken to him occasionally … probably twice a year. Even invited him to the grand opening of Precious Moments, but he didn't show though he promised he'd come. But he's been in contact with Justin in the past few days who vowed not to give him my new cell phone number. That's why I was shocked, but he sent another text while I was driving over here saying he found my number online for an advertisement for Precious Moments."

"He wants to see you now?"

"He wants my bone marrow," she answered, taking a gulp of her wine. "If I'm a match."

Dropping his fork to the plate, Blake scrunched his face in utter shock. "Wasn't expecting that answer. What's wrong with him? Cancer?"

"Yep, I can't pronounce it so please don't ask … um, something like melancholy syndrome. I haven't had a chance to research it yet."

"Myelodysplastic syndrome?"

"That's it. He wants me and Justin to see if our bone marrow matches."

"It's a possibility."

Sighing, she tossed her napkin from her lap onto her empty plate and was relieved she'd finished eating because this conversation could've made her lose her appetite.

"I don't know what to do. I hardly know the man. He hasn't exactly been a father to me. My grandfather was pretty much my father, as was Zaria's dad. He didn't even bother to show up for Justin's wedding and other important events, and now he's asking both of us to get tested to see if our bone marrow is a match. He left my mother, who in my opinion died of a broken heart! She loved him despite how he treated her." Tears welled in her eyes, and when one rushed down her cheek, Blake was right there in a hurry to wipe it off with a clean napkin along with the others that followed.

"I feel so bad saying all of that because he is my father and I do love him. I just don't love how he treated my mom and us. I do have a few fond memories with him, like going to the fair and miniature golf. I never wanted those times to end because I didn't know if I'd see him again."

"I'm sorry." He spoke softly, rubbing her back. "What can I do?"

Touching his cheek, she smiled through the tears. "That's so sweet. Asking that is enough, but I would like to know more about the type of cancer he has."

"Did he have some other type of cancer that required chemo or radiation?"

"He had prostate cancer some years ago."

"I see. Myelodysplastic syndrome sometimes develops after having treatment for another cancer as well as age or smoking. How old is your father?"

"He just turned sixty. Are there any other types of treatments besides a bone marrow transplant?"

"There's medication that will increase his white blood cells but it's not a cure. The bone marrow transplant is, and apparently, he's a candidate for it. Some patients aren't able due to other health issues or age, and have to continue with the medications or blood transfusions. Sometimes more chemo. It depends on a lot of factors."

"But there is a bone marrow registry. He can't use that?"

"Yes, but doctors do encourage immediate family members to see if they are a match providing that their health is fine. Sometimes sisters and brothers who share the same mother and father are. He doesn't have any siblings?"

"Not living."

"There have been cases where parents and children are a match. You just have to get tested. You can do it at my office if you decide, and I can have the results sent to your dad's doctor."

"At this point I haven't decided. I haven't even spoken to him yet. Justin informed me this morning. He saw my dad last night, and I guess now he wants to speak to me."

"I know this isn't easy considering you're not close to him, and he wasn't the best father in the world to you and your brother."

"Growing up without him affected my brother more than me. I was barely four when my mother died, and I remember very little of her. But Justin was twelve when she passed and at one point had a relationship with our father and then he just disappeared after my mother's death. We barely saw him except on rare occasions. I know he was in and out of jail for petty stuff, and at one point he left Memphis. Most of my anger toward him isn't even because of how he treated me, but how he treated Justin who truly wanted a father and son relationship. I need time to think before I call him back and not necessarily with an answer."

"Has Justin decided?"

"Honestly, Justin has a kind heart despite everything and the way he was speaking this morning he very well may get tested just to see. And he may actually do it if he's a match. Me? I don't know, and I feel so bad every time I say that but at the same time I want him to be okay. He is my father."

"You have a kind heart as well. One of the reasons why I'm attracted to you."

"Thank you. Enough about that." She had to change the subject. She rarely confided in the men who she was dating about her father, since it was usually a moot subject, but their growing connection made it easier. "What's for dessert?" she questioned, realizing she didn't see anything sweet on the kitchen island earlier and she could really go for something sweet as a comfort after her long day.

"Dang it." His face crumpled, and he hit his hand on his forehead. "I forgot to ask for a dessert."

"No biggie. We can think of something."

A mischievous smirk slid over his mouth. "I thought you said four months." Winking, he mouthed "just teasing."

"Very funny. I meant I can make something depending on what's in the kitchen."

Standing, he grabbed their empty dishes. "Let's take our plates down and see what's in the pantry. I always keep my nieces and nephews' favorite snacks on hand."

A few moments later, Reagan opened the refrigerator and found whip cream and strawberries. She snatched the whip cream and swished her lips to the side, shaking the can up. "Uh huh, Dr. Bachelor."

"No, it's not what you're thinking. My nieces, Lana and Bianca, like hot chocolate with whip cream."

Reagan placed it on the counter and opened the pantry. Spotting flour, sugar, and vanilla extract she grabbed all of it and set the containers on the island. "I'm going to make strawberry short cake."

"Cool. What can I do to help?"

"You can take out the mixing bowls and something to bake the cake in. You do know where all that is. Right?" she asked with a half curious smile.

"Oh sure," he answered, opening a cabinet on the island and taking out two mixing bowls, a cake pan, and a huge mixer. "My sisters are always cooking and baking when they're here."

"They live in Brunswick?" Reaching into the refrigerator, she took out the eggs, strawberries, and the milk.

"Parker and her family live in Jacksonville, Florida, but my youngest sister, Clara, and her family are in the Washington, DC area where we grew up, or at least spent our teenage years. We're military brats, but once Dad started working for the Pentagon we finally settled in one spot for awhile."

"Where you were you born?"

"Honolulu, Hawaii."

"Wow. Vacation all the time. Can you grease the cake pan for me and then cut the strawberries in half?"

"Sure. I can be your sous chef," he teased, taking the grease spray out of a nearby cabinet. "I don't remember much of Hawaii. Just going to the beach all the time and eating pineapples. I was five when we left for Germany. After Germany, it was Texas and a few other places."

"Why did you settle in Brunswick?"

"My parents are from here. They're high school sweethearts but have known each other since middle school."

"Oh, how sweet." A brief flash of Reagan's high school sweetheart appeared in her mind. She'd broken up with him before they went off to separate colleges once learning from some of her older girlfriends and cousins of how their college boyfriends would cheat on them. Reagan decided she didn't want to go through that. He was a nice guy, and she wanted to keep that image of him. She was happy that he'd found the love of his life while in grad school and she even planned their wedding in Atlanta.

"Yep, Mother says it was love at first sight … for my dad," he chuckled, cutting the strawberries. "He claims he stole her from some jock on the football team. My dad is quite the charmer and over-confident, so I can definitely see that being the case even though my mother says that's not how it happened. Anyway, he promised her they'd move back after retiring. I always enjoyed visiting my grandparents here when I was young. I'm sort of a beach bum. So after medical school I came here to do my residency. Parker followed once she graduated from college, and then my parents after they retired about three years ago. Clara's husband is from the DC area. They met at Howard and decided to stay, but they visit with my nephews often."

"That's cool. I don't know if I'd ever move back to Memphis," she commented, placing the ingredients into the mixer. "I don't miss the cold winters, but I do miss my family." Reagan stopped the mixer and unattached the bowl. He slid the pan over and she poured in the batter. "But I'm glad Zaria and Brooklyn are with me and now Addison. We didn't know her, but she fits right in."

"This batter smells good."

She nodded in agreement. "It sure does, and it's going to taste even better." She continued slowly pouring it into the cake pan." You can lick it when I'm done." As soon as she said it their eyes met in a fiery stare. Heat rose to her cheeks hotter than the glassblowing kiln, and she knew his mind was racing with all sorts of wicked thoughts. In fact, so was hers.

Blake's eyebrows rose, and he leaned over to her lips but didn't kiss her. "I bet it's just as sweet as this batter."

He stuck her finger in the almost empty bowl, then held it up as the batter dripped down her finger. He swiped his tongue over it in a seductive gesture that exaggerated her breathing and her balance. Goodness, she wanted like hell to know just how he would lick and taste another part of her that tingled with a ferocious passion that she didn't know how to turn off. Her eyelids fluttered shut and she fought to keep her composure and had almost succeeded. However, he did it a second time, lingering his hot tongue on her skin and staring at her so deep that the moan she released was quiet yet high-pitched. A heat wave swept over her body, and she clenched his shoulder tight with her free hand to stop from falling over and to compose her body that shuddered with a stimulation that could only be extinguished in one way.

Could she handle anything past his lips on her finger? *A little freaking finger.* Not her neck, breasts, or between her thighs or any other turn on spots. But just a few inches of skin that to her memory was never a turn on spot for her. She nearly laughed at herself for being this far gone, but their connection and attraction to one another had been on high since the first glance.

The third time he dipped his own finger and brought it up to her lips.

"Taste it," he demanded in a whisper.

Blake's dark, serious gaze bore into her like a hypnotic trance and only he had the command word to jerk her out of it.

"With pleasure." Reagan swirled her tongue around the tip of his finger in a slow wind, and she loved the way his breath caught in his throat. It was followed by a guttural moan as she engulfed his entire finger in her mouth, held it for a second, and slowly rose up, meeting his half-shut hazy stare. She refused to be the only one being driven insane at the moment. However, she surprised herself because she'd never felt so carefree, sensual, and comfortable with a man she'd just met to be in the position they were currently in.

"Mmm-hmm," she moaned, licking her tongue over her lips. "Delish."

The buzz of the oven to inform her that it was ready for the cake snapped both of them out of the ecstasy filled daze. Stepping away from him, she slid the pan off of the island and opened the oven, placing the cake inside.

Turning around, she found him sitting on a bar stool and licking the spoon she'd used to pour the batter. *Dang, he has a long tongue.* "The cake will be ready in about thirty minutes." She stood rooted on the other side of the island, watching the strokes of his tongue, and was disappointed when the batter was all gone.

He tossed the spoon into the mixing bowl. "Cool. You want a tour? There's more than just the kitchen and living area, you know."

"Nope," she answered quickly, catching a quick glimmer in his eye. "I'm fine right here." She playfully beat the palms of her hands on the counter.

He chuckled. "Relax. I'm not going to try anything. Besides, we can make love all over this boat. Doesn't have to just be the bedroom. The kitchen table, the island, up against the refrigerator, this bar stool, that chaise lounge up on the top deck. Shall I go on?"

Clearing her throat, she turned toward the oven to hide her wide smile and to set the timer on the oven. "No need. I'm going to clean up my mess and wait for the cake."

A phone ring from her purse sounded and she strolled over to where Blake set it earlier. Her heartbeat sped up and she prayed it wasn't her father calling her. However, she was relieved to see it was the bakery, hopefully with good news about the last-minute change for a wedding cake. She saw the concernment on Blake's face.

"I'm fine. It's the bakery," she said to him, and then pushed the accept button to answer the call. "Hey, Deidra. Please tell me you have some good news to share."

"I do," Deidra reassured in an upbeat tone. "We can change the flavor of the top layer, and add another layer to the groom's cake. I'll email you the invoice for the price change."

"Oh, wonderful. I know you don't do changes a week before the wedding, but I sincerely appreciate it."

"No problem. We want to make the bride happy."

"Thank you. She's going to be over the moon. I'll call her now."

"Perfect, Reagan. We love working with you and your clients. Have a great rest of the evening."

"Thank you. You too."

Reagan quickly called the bride, relayed the good news, and then rejoined Blake in the kitchen. He was setting the dishes in the dishwasher with his back to her and she couldn't help but stare at his butt, which fit nice and snug in his black slacks.

"Everything worked out for your client?"

"Yep. She's a happy camper, and by this time next week she'll be on her honeymoon in Paris, but she doesn't know that."

"Surprise from her future husband?"

"Yes, she thinks they're going to Myrtle Beach. She's going to be so ecstatic."

"So honeymoons are something the groom takes care of. Right?"

"Grooms typically plan the honeymoon and a few other things. It just depends on how traditional the couple is, age, money, and ..." She paused, wondering if his mother's assistant had witnessed their sexy moment earlier. Reagan had forgotten they weren't alone. "Where's Kara?"

"She was only here to set the ambiance and left right after she served the food. Her granddaughter had a dance recital this evening."

"Oh." It had just dawned on her that they were apparently alone but she didn't mind. She was comfortable with Blake. "The cake should be done soon. Can we eat up on the top deck?"

"That sounds like a plan. I'll meet you up there. I just need to do my Sunday night conference call with my assistant. It shouldn't take long."

"Can't wait."

Chapter Seven

The phrase "can't wait" seemed to be Reagan's favorite words to say to Blake, and while today was no exception, she was a lot more apprehensive. When he'd mentioned setting up a meeting with his mother about the anniversary dinner party, it dawned on Reagan that she was going to meet his mother. She even uttered the favorite phrase. And while it was supposed to be a work-related, professional meeting, as with any client, she was nervous. However, she kept it bottled inside for the last hour as they discussed the event, and prayed Mrs. Harrison didn't realize that deep down she was mentally gnawing on her fingernails.

"Since pink and green are your favorite colors, I think this sage green will mesh well with this blush pink for the color scheme. And the flower arrangements Zaria has envisioned are over the top." Reagan clicked the next button on the computer screen of her presentation with a sketch of the centerpieces made up of calla lilies, pink tulips, and an assortment of other white flowers.

"This is splendid!" Mrs. Harrison exclaimed, clapping her hands as her brown eyes that matched Blake's brightened. "Just splendid."

It had been two weeks since her houseboat dinner date with Blake. She'd seen him several times since then, which was a lot for her considering her busy schedule. However, every moment spent with him was relaxing, fun, and serene. Today was no different as they'd cooked Sunday brunch together on his houseboat followed by stopping by his parents' home so she could meet with them about their anniversary dinner. She'd already spoken to his father over the phone about the secret vow renewal, but other than that, whatever his wife wanted he didn't mind. And besides introducing himself to her, he nor his son were present during the meeting. Instead, it was just her and Mrs. Harrison sitting in a huge rounded, Florida room surrounded by indoor plants hanging from the ceiling, two cockatoos on a huge, man-made tree type of structure, and a row of two-story windows facing the ocean.

"Thank you, Mrs. Harrison."

"And thank you. I've already met with Chef Walter about the menu, so seeing the layout and the centerpieces, it's really coming together. So happy that my son recommended you to assist me. My daughters were, but they're not professionals and with two preteens each, their time was tight for them."

"My pleasure." Reagan smiled sweetly at Blake's refined and graceful mother. She was the epitome of style, charm, and elegance. Even on a casual Sunday afternoon, Mrs. Harrison was impeccably dressed in an off-white pants suit accented with diamond stud earrings and a tennis bracelet graced her right wrist. Her short gray hair was styled in a pixie cut that offset her smooth cocoa face. Not a single wrinkle except for two laugh lines on her cheeks when she smiled.

"So, Blake tells me you're from Memphis." Mrs. Harrison swiped a wisp of hair from her forehead and smiled pleasantly. "My husband and I went there once years ago for a wedding of some classmates of ours from college. Loved the blues clubs on Beale Street. Is your family still there?"

"Yes. My brother and his family, and uncles and cousins." It was on the tip of her tongue to say and my father, but she couldn't spill it out. Since his text messages, she hadn't responded, but she did inform Justin and told him she needed more time. He had made up his mind to get tested and scheduled an appointment for the following week. In the meantime, their father's doctor was searching for a donor through the registry as well.

"Wonderful. I'm sure they're all very proud of you." Pausing, Mrs. Harrison poured herself another glass of lemonade. "Sooooooo … you and my son are a thing? Am I right?"

While Blake said he didn't disclose to his parents that they were dating, he did introduce her as a very special friend. He'd then proceeded to kiss her cheek before he and his father had left the sunroom to watch a basketball game. She'd noted the inquisitive eye raise his mother had displayed at the gesture, but Reagan had to brush it aside to get through their meeting.

Trying hard not to blush as her lips pressed together, Reagan laughed lightly. She really hated meeting the parents so early on in a relationship, and in fact hadn't met the mothers of the last three guys she'd dated but probably because none of them had made it past three months. The one who made it to six months, his parents lived in New York.

Reagan decided to tell the truth since it was rather obvious. "Yes, we've been on a couple of dates for the past few weeks."

"I saw the way he looked at you. You know, Blake never brings home women that he isn't serious about, so I guess we will be seeing a lot more of you. You should come with us next weekend on our family outing. The grandkids love water sports and so do my children. I love being on the water … but in the boat watching from the deck sipping wine. How about you?"

"I prefer to relax on the beach, soak in the sun, and read a book. However, I also enjoy water sports. Just depends on my mood."

"I swear I birthed fish not babies, but they used to visit here most summers to spend time with their grandparents. I hope you're able to join us."

"Yes. Blake invited me since I finally have a Saturday off."

"Splendid." Pausing, Mrs. Harrison perused the room as if she had a secret to tell, then leaned over the table to Reagan. "You know I'm aware of the vow renewal ceremony the General is planning." Winking with an amused smirk, she sat upright in the outdoor wicker chair and sipped her lemonade.

Reagan's heart dropped down to her wedge sandals. She had to put her professional cap back on in a jiffy. Mrs. Harrison had started to make her feel comfortable and personable discussing the weekend outing. "I don't know anything about a vow renewal, Mrs. Harrison. We're only planning a dinner party."

"Sweetie, please call me Ms. Lola. No one calls me Mrs. Harrison. Now I know you've been sworn to secrecy by my husband; however, my daughters informed me. They had to, and I'm glad they did. The dress I was contemplating would've been all wrong. No worries. I just wanted you to know I know, just in case my husband suggests something outlandish that I would never go for. Luckily, my daughters have reassured me they gave him some pointers. I'm sure you'll steer him in the right direction."

Reagan kept a straight face and said with ease, "Whatever you say, Mrs. Harrison … I mean, Ms. Lola."

"Just know that the General may have had his top secret job at the Pentagon, but in this household, he can't keep any secrets from me. So about my dress. Or rather dresses. I'm going to New York in a few weeks to visit a stylist girlfriend of mine who I used to work with in the fashion industry eons ago. But my husband doesn't know that I'm also going to Elle Lauren's Showroom for a cocktail dress and a wedding gown fitting."

"Oh, Elle's dresses are to die for and she's fun to work with."

"You know her?"

"I've met her a few times. She's married to my sister-in-law's cousin, Braxton Chase, the jazz pianist."

"Yes, I heard all about the surprise proposal he gave her after a fashion show in front of everyone considering he'd left her at the altar over a decade ago. Wish I could've been present. I attended her first fashion show years ago when I was a fashion editor. She was an upcoming powerhouse and is now a stable pillar in the wedding design world."

"I saw her last month at Braxton's cousin's wedding in Atlanta. Elle designed the bridal party attire."

"Is that the wedding where Zaria said everyone that wanted to could skydive with the bride and groom as they were married, including the couple's golden retrievers?"

"Yes, but I observed from the ground. They also had a traditional ceremony and reception that afternoon. It was a fun-filled, romantic day for Preston and Blythe."

"That's awesome. I don't think the General could've gotten me to agree to do that. I'm not a dare devil and terrified of heights. However, eloping without my parents' knowledge or permission was indeed scary, but I loved him and would do it all again. That's why I'm excited about—" Mrs. Harrison halted as her attention was drawn to a light knock on the French doors behind Reagan. Clearing her throat, she gave Reagan a knowing glance. "Here are our handsome men now."

Turning her head, Reagan's gaze met Blake's with a humorous twinkle at his mother's words. Reagan tried to ignore the statement but it was no use. The thought of

Blake actually being her man stayed imprinted on her brain for the rest of the day and into the night as she laid in the bed wide awake. The notion of such hadn't crossed her mind, but it was like having another duh or but-of-course moment which placed fear in her once more. She wasn't necessarily scared of him breaking her heart, but of their magnetic connection that didn't compare to any other relationship she'd been in. Normally she was on guard and searching for signals and red flags that she felt her mother didn't catch with her father. However, with Blake, she found herself yearning to know everything that made him the enduring and intelligent man he was. Upon meeting his parents, some of her questions were answered. He had an astute and commanding presence like the General that automatically demanded respect. He also possessed Mrs. Harrison's sense of humor and giving spirit as both were involved with numerous charities.

The light from her cell phone lit up the dark room. Swiping it from the nightstand, she squinted to read a text from Blake stating that he had an early morning appointment with a patient and wouldn't be jogging on the beach during her yoga class. Sighing, she sent back a sad face and flopped back against the pillows. Scrolling through her text message list, she came across the ones her father had sent asking her to call him. It had been two weeks and she didn't know how much longer she could put off the inevitable. Taking a deep breath, she pushed the number as her heart stopped beating. *What the heck did I just do?* She didn't even know how she was going to speak for there was a huge nervous block stuck in her throat.

Maybe there's still time to hang up.

He answered on the second ring in an upbeat yet somewhat surprised tone.

"Baby girl," he paused as a relieved sigh breathed out, "I'm so glad you called."

Reagan remained silent for a moment. She wasn't expecting him to answer so soon and had almost hung up as edginess crept along her skin.

"Reagan? Are you there?" he asked, sounding like an older version of Justin. It was uncanny how both of them looked and sounded just alike, including their mannerisms even though they were rarely around each other.

Sliding the comforter back, she jumped out of the bed and turned on the lamp before settling into her chaise lounge with her grandmother's quilt for comfort. Even though the thought of rushing to the kitchen for a glass of wine would definitely help as well.

"Hey ..." She wanted to say Dad or Father but couldn't. While she always referred to him as such to others, she'd never called him anything in his presence except when she was a little girl. She wasn't going to do like Justin and sarcastically refer to him as Mr. Brown when speaking directly to him. "Am I calling you too late? Its ten o'clock here."

"No. I'm a night owl. I guess you got that from me."

She chuckled. "No ... I'm not a night owl. Justin is. I just couldn't sleep. A lot on my mind lately."

"I'm sorry about that. I know finding out that I have cancer again and would like for you and your brother to see if your bone marrow matches mine isn't easy. Trust me, it wasn't easy to ask, but like I told Justin, I understand if you decide not to find out if your bone marrow is a match. I haven't exactly been the world's greatest dad."

"No you haven't, but at the end of the day we're family. I just hate that we aren't closer."

"That's my fault. I take full responsibility and I hope this will bring us closer. I pray you can find it in your heart to one day to forgive me for everything. I know you hate me and I understand, but I do love you. Always have."

She was silent for a moment, processing those familiar words from him. They seemed to have the same conversation every few years. However, most of the time she'd listen and then hurry up and get off the phone, or if it was in person, she'd changed the subject to a neutral conversation.

"I don't hate you," she said honestly. "However, at one point in my life I think I did, or maybe it was that I hated the way you treated my mother and Justin. I hate the situation that you put us in. I expect men to be men and take care of their responsibilities like my grandfather and my uncles and now my brother. Just because you and my mother couldn't get along it doesn't mean you had to punish your children. We're your flesh and blood obviously or you wouldn't have asked Justin and I to check to see if our bone marrow matches yours."

"I'm sorry for that. I truly am."

Reagan thought about the usual hanging up or moving on to another topic. Though a part of her needed him to know how she truly felt in order to have a peace of mind and closure before she could move any further in even considering having her bone marrow tested for him.

"This isn't the first time we've had this conversation. You've apologized before, promised you'd be in our lives and then disappeared like we don't mean anything to you. Yes, I know you've reached out prior to your cancer diagnosis and I've ignored you. I was tired of the broken record speech and you keep making and breaking promises. Its hurtful. The only reason why I'm calling you now is that you are my father, and I do care about you despite everything."

"Well, I appreciate you taking the time to call me. Even if you don't decide to get tested, it doesn't matter."

"I haven't fully made up my mind. I'm somewhat on the fence. A part of me is feeling used at the moment, because the only reason you've reached out to us is that you're desperate. But the other part as your daughter and as a human being is to hear you out and see what can be done. I'd feel guilty if I could've helped in any way and didn't."

"You definitely have your mother's kind heart and spirit. I hate she didn't see you grow up to be the beautiful, independent woman you are."

Reagan had to do a double-take at the phone and restrain herself from cursing him out, but her blood was boiling and for once she didn't care about his feelings.

"You didn't see me grow up either and don't tell me again you keep up with me from afar. I've heard it before. I'm not calling you to rehash the past. I know I've ignored you at times because you weren't there for us growing up, and now sometimes I don't feel as if I need you in my life because I didn't have you then and I turned out pretty okay."

"And you did. Your grandparents did a fantastic job raising you and your brother. If you had been with me, I can't promise you would've had the same upbringing and opportunities that you had, baby girl. You remind me of your mother in some ways with your spunk and the independent nature that you possess."

"Well, you're right. I have grown into an independent woman. Almost *too* independent. I hate men trying to take care of me or control me because I don't trust them, and I can take care of Reagan Richardson just fine. But I find myself searching for any little reason or red flag to dump men before they dump me because I don't want to be heartbroken or feel abandoned. Zaria and my friends say it's because I have daddy issues, and as much as I try to deny that, I know it's true. And in order to move on I have to know somewhere in that horrible messed up mind of yours you do love me even though you weren't around to show it."

"It's not that I didn't want to be around, I just didn't feel as if I could give you and your brother the best life poss—"

"Yeah, yeah," she said with sarcasm as she cut off what she was sure of the same old speech. "You had your reasons. Yes, I know you were in and out of jail at one point for petty robbery and drug dealing. Yes, I know you moved to another state for a job opportunity and yes, I know that at one point before my mother died, she forbade you to see us. But a real man would've pushed all that aside to be there for his children that needed him. Even if you couldn't raise us on your own as a single dad, you could've done so much more. My grandparents, including your own mother, were older, almost retired and already had raised their children. You didn't think that perhaps paying child support or taking us on the weekends could've helped them out?"

"Reagan, I know I messed up. I know I wasn't the best father to you and I have felt guilty about that every day of my life. I'm truly sorry for hurting you and Justin. And it isn't a recent feeling … its all the time."

"You can stop with the apologies. I've forgiven you, but not for you. I've forgiven you for me or I'd be miserable for the rest of my life, and despite not having you in it, I have a wonderful life. Tonight I needed to get rid of all of what has been bottled up for nearly thirty years out or I'd never be able to think rationally when it comes to you. So you don't need to apologize anymore. You want to be in my life? Fine. You don't? That's fine, too. Now as far as the test, I'll let you know soon."

"I'm truly sorry for hurting you. I know you needed to get it off your chest. And I'm here if you need to release more."

"Nope. I'm fine now." Tears began to well in her eyes and her voice would begin to crack if they talked any longer. "It's late and I have an early morning, but I'll be in contact."

"I appreciate it. Good night, baby girl."

"Good night."

Reagan quickly hung up the call and closed her eyes as the hot tears finally fell. She was relieved she was able to rid her brain and heart of everything she'd thought about her father over the years. While she felt somewhat better,

Reagan didn't know if he truly understood and would make an effort to be in her life.

Glancing at the cell phone screen, she spotted a text message alert box. Blake had sent a text message ten minutes ago and her phone was sending a reminder. She'd vaguely remembered hearing a beep but had ignored it because she was spilling to her father. Pushing the box on the touch screen, she read the message from Blake.

Have a great night, babe. Sweet dreams.

Good night as well. Just received your message. I finally called my father.

Instead of a message back, the phone in her hand began to ring and the picture she snapped of Blake's handsome face posing on his houseboat from that morning appeared on her screen.

"Hey, Reagan. Are you alright?"

"Um … well … uh …yes and no."

"Tell me what happened."

She gave him a rundown of the conversation with her father that sounded more like a rant, and she found herself even more frustrated.

"I'm proud of you, Reagan. I know that had to be hard, but you're a strong woman. One of the traits I admire about you."

The tears started again, but this time they were uncontrollable as the emotions causing the heaviness that had been on her heart for years were finally being lifted.

"Babe, I hate that you're crying because I'm not there to console and hold you," Blake said in a comforting manner. "But I can come right now. I'm still on my houseboat, so I'm ten minutes away from St. Simons."

Sniffing, she smiled briefly and dried her eyes on the quilt. "No, that's so sweet but you don't have to. Its late. I'll be fine. This is something I have to deal with."

"I want to, though. If you need me I'll be there. You don't have to go through this by yourself."

"Okay. I'd love for you to come. I don't want to be alone right now."

"Text me your address."

Chapter Eight

Twenty minutes later, Blake pulled into the driveway of Reagan's craftsmen-styled ranch home that also served as the Precious Moments Events place of business. There was a classy, pink wooden sign with the company name at the edge of the driveway which was flanked with an abundance of spring flowers and solar spotlights on either side. She'd instructed him to follow the driveway around to the back of the house as that was her home entrance. The front door was for clients.

Normally he didn't stay at the houseboat on Sunday nights, but he had an early morning appointment with a patient who lived on the island. His home was on the outskirts of Brunswick and would've taken him forty minutes to drive to the island depending upon traffic. Now, he was relieved in his decision as his concernment for Reagan filled him. It broke his heart to hear her cry, and he felt helpless on the phone because he needed to hold her. When he'd offered to come over, he'd expected her to say no because of her dating rule of not letting men know where she lived early in the relationship. And he respected that, but he needed to see her. The need to comfort her weighed heavy on him. He wanted to take away her pain and transfer it to him. Blake swore he heard a tad of shock in her voice when she said okay, and at first he thought her text message would probably be a change of mind not her address.

Blake parked next to a white Lexus GX 460 SUV with the company's logo imprinted on the driver's side. A motion light popped on and blanketed the area, causing his gaze to shift to Reagan standing on the wrap-around porch. Her swollen face and puffy, blood-shot eyes saddened him for a bit, but he was there to cheer her up. Putting on a bright and sincere smile, he exited the vehicle and began to walk briskly toward her.

Gathering her in his arms, he held Reagan close to his chest and she relaxed against him in a relieved exhale.

"Hey, sweetheart," Blake greeted, cupping her chin and gently kissing her lips.

"Thank you for coming," she said with a sniff.

"No need to thank me, darling. I just want to make you feel better."

Reagan slid from his embrace and stepped aside so he could trail her into the house. Once she secured the locks and set the alarm, she motioned for him to follow her from the mudroom which led to a small sunroom off from the kitchen. Blake tried to keep his focus and remember why he was there, but watching her hips sway while her butt bounced under the blue silk material caused a stir in his groin.

Shoving his hands in his pants pockets to keep them from ripping off her nightgown, Blake studied the room briefly as the tranquil furnishings fit her whimsical personality. A plush, comfy beige couch sat in the corner with an antique wood table in front of it. A clear vase filled with fresh-cut yellow and red tulips sat on the table along with wedding books and magazines. Behind the couch was a collage of photos all in pretty, adorned jeweled frames. One caught his eye of her and who he assumed was her brother—for they had the same smile and curly hair except her hair was sandy brown—at her college graduation. The couch was in the perfect position as it faced a window seat lined with an assortment of pillows, and its backdrop was a bay window framing the moon and stars which shone on the Atlantic Ocean.

To his right was the galley kitchen. It was small, and while it was in need of updating as she'd mentioned to him while they cooked brunch that morning on his houseboat, her touches of fine china and crystal wine glasses on the counter reminded him of her refined elegance. A round glass table with four wicker chairs was in the eating area. He smiled as he saw the bowl she'd created on their first date which contained lemons and limes.

"Do you want anything to eat or drink?" She nodded her head toward a black tea kettle sitting on the stove. "I'm going to make some tea."

Drawing her to him once more, he shook his head. "No. I came to comfort you. You relax on the couch and I'll make it. Just tell me where everything is located."

Ten minutes later, he handed Reagan a cup of chamomile tea and plopped next to her on the couch. He watched her slowly sip the warm liquid and breathe in deeply.

"Thank you. This is good. Just the right amount of honey."

"Perfect."

"You're sweet," she said, touching the palm of her hand to his face in a tender way. "I feel bad you came over here so late and you have an early appointment."

"Nonsense. I'm a doctor. I'm used to staying up late and having to be up early in the morning and do it all over again. Comes with the job."

"But you own a private practice. Don't you make your own hours?"

"Yep, but emergencies don't have designated hours and I'm a concierge doctor. Some of my patients have access to me almost 24/7."

Setting the tea cup on the wooden table in front of the couch, Reagan scooted closer to him and nuzzled her head on his chest. "I appreciate you coming over."

"If you need to talk or cry again, that's what I'm here for, sweetie."

"No … just hold me," she said barely above a whisper.

Wrapping his arms around her, he gently swayed them back in forth in a soothing rhythm, reminding him of their salsa lesson. They were quiet for awhile as he placed tender, comforting kisses on her forehead and cheeks. Sometimes she giggled, sometimes she'd glance up at him and crack a half smile or snuggle even closer against him which he didn't think was even possible.

Moments later he heard a soft snore and realized the tea, and hopefully him, had relaxed Reagan to sleep. Readjusting them until she was laying on top of him, he kissed her forehead and drifted into a peaceful sleep as well.

Blake felt a tapping on his shoulder and a sweet, groggy voice whispering his name over and over. He knew he was in a deep sleep. Almost coma-like. Warm and comfortable. He was in a place of serenity, and the angelic voice that continued rolling his name off her lips was the sweetest music he'd ever heard. Opening his eyes, his stare landed on gorgeous yet concerned ginger eyes that indeed belonged to an angel.

"Hey, sleepy head," Reagan said, gliding her body off of his, but he snatched her back to him.

"Mmm … where you going, woman?"

"Apparently nowhere." She snickered lightly. "But it's a little after twelve-thirty. That tea put us to sleep. Or maybe it was you rocking me like a baby."

"Well, you are my baby."

She rubbed her nose against his before sitting up and retreating to the other side of the couch while stretching her arms out above her head. "What time is your appointment?" she inquired, yawning.

I guess she's kicking me out. It was for the best considering the amorous ideas that had crossed his mind when she was on top of him with her breasts pressed against his chest. The thought of pulling down the top part of her nightgown to suck and lick on her caramel mounds caused a tight strain against his boxer briefs. He sat all the way up in a swift jerk and glanced at his keys on the kitchen counter.

Yep, it was time to go. "Seven. Not too far from here. My patient lives by the Village Pier area."

"Stay here tonight. I don't want you driving back to Brunswick only to come back in a few hours. I know you keep your medical bag secured in the trunk of your car."

Glancing at the softness of her skin and the strap of her gown, which had slipped past her shoulder, the urge to slip the other one down until the entire negligee puddled at her feet was playing in his head over and over. "Not a good idea." He couldn't believe he'd uttered those words.

"Why not? You don't trust me?" She winked, running her hand up his jeans. "Scared I may seduce you?"

Grabbing her hand, he brought it to his lips and kissed it. "Bring it," he teased her, but in his head he was quite serious.

"I was joking. You know my rule."Tilting her head to the side, a wicked smirk smoothed up her cheeks. "But we can do other things."

Rising from her spot, Reagan straddled his lap. He placed his hands on her hips and pushed all the way down so she could feel how excited he was of her in that position. Goodness, he wanted her to really feel him especially when he trailed his hands to her bottom and discovered she wasn't wearing any panties. While he figured she was like some women who didn't sleep in underwear, at the same time he couldn't but halfway hope it was an invitation. Still, he needed to be strong as his desire for her grew stronger with everyday of her being in his life. It was a newfound feeling that he couldn't remember with any other woman. She was perfect, and the fact that she was in his arms and that she trusted him enough not to try to break her rule, caused him to fall for her even more.

Reagan kissed the side of his neck and licked around to his ear before landing her mouth on his for a deep, seductive kiss which caused a groan to rise from his throat. She mimicked it in an arrogant way as if she was pleased with herself for turning him on. Winding his tongue around hers in a sensual, unhurried rhythm, Blake didn't know how much longer he could put himself through the pleasant torture of restraint. Her breasts pressed against his chest and her center lightly grinded on him as she continued her tongue journey along his neck and collarbone and back around to his ear.

"Mmm ... I don't know if that's a great idea." He couldn't believe those words had come out his mouth yet again, but he wanted to be respectful of her rule. "For the record, I want all of you ..." He groaned as she nibbled little bites on the side of his neck. "Which is why ... shit, you feel good ...um ... I should leave." He flung her satin hair cap across the room and wove his hands into her thick tresses.

She moaned a pout. "I don't want to be alone tonight."

"And I don't want you to be."

Rising off of him, she held out her hand. "Then don't go."

*****

Did I really just say that?

Reagan questioned herself as she led him to her bedroom. No, she wasn't going to have sex with him. They'd established that wasn't going to happen yet, though usually she tried to avoid even the possibility by not entertaining the other options. However, she needed to feel her body next to his. She craved for his lips to kiss her wherever his tongue decided to travel on her skin. She'd never considered herself a prude and had always enjoyed the intimate side of her relationships, but it was rare that she would seduce a man the way she had on the couch. Her willpower had weakened thanks to the moment he'd stepped out of his Escalade and rushed to comfort her. It was indeed a turn on that he was concerned about her well-being late at night when he had an early morning appointment and probably needed to rest.

Though now as Blake backed her up against the wall by the chaise lounge and sucked one of her breasts into his mouth, she decided some rules could be broken. She sounded a long, satisfied moan that he must have enjoyed hearing for he moved his mouth over to the other breast and did the exact same tantalizing act. His tongue circled around her nipples back and forth as one of his hands held her hands above her head and the other massaged whichever breast he wasn't driving crazy.

Her knees turned into jelly as she found herself shaking with delight at the possibility of where his tongue would end up. Gripping his hand that held both of hers, Reagan squirmed to keep her balance. But the passionate rush bolting through her veins and to her center made it hard to stand still. She decided to give up considering this wasn't yoga and the need to stay balanced wasn't necessary.

Reagan was in awe that this was happening. The angels on her shoulder had been arguing over what she should do and she sided with the naughty one. Reagan tried to chalk it up to being upset about her conversation with her father and probably vulnerable. However, she knew that wasn't the case. Blake had rattled unexplored territories in her mind and heart since she'd first met him. There was an air of intrigue and charm that made him sexy even with simple tasks such as making her tea. She'd watched him while he made the effort to brew it just as she'd instructed with a one teaspoon of honey, water, and two tea bags.

Now he was driving her up a wall, literally, while unraveling all the ways she normally kept her guard up.

Her moans were intensified each time his lips and hands handled her in a way that made her aware she was indeed a woman who was being spoiled for the first time ever with passion and desire. When he released his hand on hers, he brought them around his neck and proceeded to slide the straps of her nightgown off until it landed on her bamboo floor.

Blake stood away from her and raked his eyes slowly over her body. Reagan found herself becoming self aware of imperfections in her opinion that she'd never thought about with a man before. The little mole just above her belly button and the scar that never healed properly on her left thigh when she'd fell on roller skates as a teenager. Then there was the splotch on her back from an allergic breakout last summer which was why she hadn't worn a backless dress since.

He settled his eyes on hers and ran a finger along her cheek. "You're beautiful. I'm sure you've heard that before, huh?" he asked, raising an eyebrow.

Wrinkling her forehead, she contemplated for a moment. "Honestly, yes, but its more special coming from you. It's like I've never been told that before now. Can't explain it. It's almost a surreal emotion. I feel like I'm having a lot of firsts with you even though that's not true."

"Mmm … maybe because you've fallen for me just like I've fallen for you."

"Oh really? You think I've fallen for you?" she quipped, lifting her chin as a half-grin emerged. "You got it like that, Doc?"

"Apparently. You're standing in front of me in your fine ass birthday suit and just finished the most complex symphony of moans and I haven't even gotten started yet. That was just a tease, Reagan."

"Well, keep teasing."

"My pleasure."

A sinfully sexy smirk inched up his left cheek, nearly snatching Reagan's breath away. Perhaps she'd spoken too soon. Perhaps she should've suggested they'd gone too far, and he should make his way to the guestroom while she barricaded herself in her bedroom so she wouldn't escape to sprint to him because she didn't know how much restraint she had left. However, when his lips captured hers, all of her thoughts were just nonsensical mumbo jumbo and flew out the window that she shut hard and locked.

There was nothing wrong with having a little lustful fun with the man who made her more aware of her senses. Blake was definitely easy on the eyes with his inviting smile and eyes that mesmerized her like a hypnotist. He smelled of warm citrus with fresh apple pie mixed with his own intoxicating all-man scent. Listening to him was indeed a treat for no matter what he said his deep, baritone voice was like a seductive symphony that always caused a fervent crescendo to crash through her body. Then there was the way he handled her with enduring, possessive hands, making her his with every single sensual touch. The more he caressed and kissed her, the more she lost the memory of the men before him. To taste him … mmm … just the very essence of her lips on him was like savoring a scrumptious piece of chocolate cake that she knew she shouldn't keep eating but couldn't help herself. She wanted all of it.

"Mmm … why are you so damn amazing?" Blake asked, cascading his tongue down her body until he reached her belly button. "You're so perfect."

"Thanks, but have you not noticed my scars or the tad bit of cellulite on my thighs that won't go away now that I'm over thirty despite working out?"

Clutching her hips, he lightly kissed her stomach. "Nonsense. You have a beautiful body, but an even more beautiful spirit."

She was relieved he didn't continue kissing her stomach because she was ticklish in that spot and would end up on the floor laughing hysterically, killing their current amorous mood.

"Thank you," she whispered. Her breathing was slowly becoming unhinged as she anticipated where he was headed. The wait was short-lived as he kissed her inner thighs while gently massaging her bottom. "Goodness ... Blake ..." Her pulsed raced as he teased his tongue along her thighs while the build-up continued. When he circled a finger around her middle, a pleasured moan erupted and her legs shook. She didn't know how much longer she could stand against the wall without tumbling down it. Reagan's answer came when he replaced his finger with a gentle lick of his tongue, sending a swift wave of scorching desire to crash through her. Blake caught her effortlessly as she lost her balance. Lifting her up, he laid her on the chaise lounge and proceeded to kneel in front of her, never missing a single beat of the rhythm he created with his lips and tongue.

Heat and desire pulsated through her body and the moans of ecstasy exploded from her. She couldn't catch her breath. It was as though she was running a marathon when all she was doing was lying down and enjoying Blake's lethal tongue dance. She whispered his name over and over like a broken record but it was the only word she knew at the moment.

Grasping his head, he sank deeper inside of her as her hips began to rotate in the same tempo. She was falling into a pleasant abyss of rapture that she didn't want to end and the more he licked the more she wanted ... no, needed him.

"Please, Blake," she screeched.

"Please what?"

"Make love to me," she said breathlessly as she stared at him through hazy eyes.

"We can't as much as I want to, babe. We can't. Trust me, I'm having a hard time saying this."

"Why not?"

"For one, it's not time, and two, I don't have any condoms. And I don't have any because it's not time."

Reagan sat all the way up. "But I want you now, and I have condoms left over from a bachelorette party. The bride gave them as prank gifts. They're in my office which is right on the other side of that door." She nodded toward her office.

"Um … babe, what kind are they?"

"What do you mean what kind? I don't know. Just condoms."

Blake snickered lightly and dragged her hand down to his pants. "You think they'd fit?"

She felt the hardness of him and realized what he meant. "Oh … um … no. They're just regular sized and you seem to be not so regular."

"Condoms are not one size fits all." He took her hand and brought it to his lips. "Besides, when we make love, I don't want you in a vulnerable state. I want you focused solely on us. No interruptions. No time restraints or other commitments. Plus, once we make love, no turning back. No running away from me. I have to know you're ready for us because I want you to be all mine."

Reagan nodded her head, knowing Blake was right because she was still in a vulnerable state from her conversation with her father. Though the way Blake had comforted her, she didn't want it to end, and the urge to be one with him was greater than any emotion she'd ever experienced for a man. As she laid tight in his embrace moments later in bed, the thought of being all his sent a blissful current through her, and in her heart she knew that's exactly what she craved. To be all his.

Chapter Nine

The smile plastered on Reagan's face could not be erased as she reminisced about the previous night with Blake. Even though they hadn't gone all the way, she still felt as though they'd made love and the notion of doing so sent a warm shiver across her skin. Their time together had been passionate, magical, and emotional. Her desire and connection with him was on a level she hadn't experienced before. It took all the willpower she had not to beg the man to have sex even after he said they should wait. She'd craved every bit of his tempting body and the way he'd caressed her skin with his hands along with his hot tongue that surely left burn marks on her.

"You know, you keep smiling like that and your face is going to grow into the Joker's."

Zaria's sassy remark pulled Reagan out of her daydream and back to the Monday brunch meeting that had wrapped up ten minutes ago. The ladies had been discussing Addison's upcoming camping trip in her mobile tiny house and Reagan had tuned them out as her thoughts led her back to the man whose name she couldn't stop panting the night before.

Brooklyn swished her lips to the side in a mischievous grin. "Yes, seems like someone has been in a blissful daze since meeting the man of her dreams."

"We're having a nice time learning about each other," Reagan admitted, taking the last bite of her blueberry pancake.

"Yep ... we can tell you are having a grand time together." Zaria pointed at Reagan's neck. "There's a little red bite mark to prove it. You hate love bites. Does he have a matching one?" she asked, with a pursed smirk.

Frowning, Reagan rubbed the spot her cousin referred to and was embarrassed they'd noticed. She'd purposely placed her hair in a side ponytail to cover it. And her cousin was right. She'd hated having hickies on her neck and usually stopped a man if he attempted to place one on her considering she was over twenty. With Blake, it felt absolutely mind-boggling and stopping him wasn't on the agenda.

"No, he doesn't have a matching one," she replied, with an amused eye-roll. "But anyway, he's a really great guy and I'm enjoying being with him. We spent majority of yesterday together. I met his parents and went over the details with his mother for the anniversary party. Mrs. Harrison loved your centerpiece ideas, Zaria."

"Met the parents?" Addison questioned, as she glanced down at her cell phone and began typing. "Sounds serious. Rather early in the relationship. Men don't introduce just anybody to their parents, especially the mothers." She pouted at the phone and excused herself in a dart to the kitchen.

Reagan glanced after Addison who was usually in a cheery mood and hoped it wasn't anything too serious.

"I agree with Addison, my dear friend," Brooklyn interjected. "When was the last time you met someone's mother this early in the relationship?"

"No, I'm not reading too much into that. I had to meet with her about the anniversary party." Even though as she said it, Reagan remembered his mother's words: 'Blake never brings home women that he isn't serious about.' They'd played in her head for the rest of the day as she'd contemplated just how serious they were becoming. And when he'd showed up later that night to check on her, she knew their relationship was going down that road. Part of it scared her while the other part was looking forward to the ride.

"You know we love to give time limits on your relationships since you're good at dumping men within the first few months," Brooklyn said, standing and collecting the empty plates. "But I think we may be planning your wedding after all."

Zaria took the last swig of her orange juice and began to assist Brooklyn with the dishes. "Congrats. You're no longer the wedding planner that will never marry. Maybe now you can start actually visualizing your own wedding."

Reagan laughed at their comments. Though she could visualize not only a wedding but actually being married to Blake. She'd never been a woman to dream of her fairy tale wedding even as a little girl because she didn't know who she was going to marry and therefore didn't see the point. As a wedding planner, during her first meeting with a couple, she'd listen to their ideas of what they've always envisioned and then pull from them their likes and tastes together in order to incorporate all of it into a magical, unique wedding just for the bride and groom.

She didn't want to admit to Brooklyn and Zaria that thanks to the first kiss with Blake and the taste of his coffee ice cream on her lips, that she wanted an ice cream station at her wedding reception. The idea had leapt into her brain immediately along with other little things along the way such as a beach wedding in the same spot where they'd met.

Grabbing the serving dishes, Reagan followed the ladies inside to the kitchen where Addison sat at the kitchen table with a slight frown.

"What's wrong, hon?" Brooklyn asked.

"I just received a text message from Chase. He's not coming next week because I told him I'd be busy with the festivities planned for the spring breakers. That didn't mean I wouldn't be available to chill with him. But I guess it's okay. I'm going home soon and he'll be here for a few months this fall teaching a pre-law course at the University of North Florida."

Reagan couldn't help but glance at Brooklyn who she knew had secretly hoped to see Chase. Addison had convinced him to stay with her in her tiny house which was parked in Brooklyn's backyard. Reagan had hoped that perhaps her friend would actually hold a conversation with him and maybe even pursue the innocent crush into something more. Reagan had noted the way Chase followed Brooklyn around the reception hall with his eyes the last time they were all together at his cousin Preston's wedding. She'd seemed flattered with his obvious attraction to her.

Reagan noticed the disappointment in her friend's eyes as their gazes met. As much as Brooklyn tried to deny and protest that she didn't have a crush on Chase, a picture always spoke a thousand words.

"How long is the course?" Reagan asked even though she was really asking for Brooklyn whose eyebrow had raised when Addison had mentioned him teaching the class at the university which was an hour from Brunswick in Jacksonville, Florida.

"I believe the entire semester." Addison shrugged. "Which would be awesome, but I'm not sure if he'll want to stay with me in my little home the entire time. The guest loft isn't that comfortable for long term and he's so tall, he makes my place seem like a broom closet."

"Maybe he can find an apartment near campus or he can stay with Brooklyn," Zaria suggested. "That way you can still be near him, Addy."

The rattling of dishes turned everyone's attention to Brooklyn as she rinsed the plates before setting them in the dishwasher. Reagan was the only one of the ladies who knew of Brooklyn's attraction to Chase.

"Usually colleges have temporary housing for visiting professors," Reagan said, hoping to put her best friend at ease. She decided to change the subject fast so her grandmother's china wouldn't end up shattered on the floor, especially when she noticed Brooklyn's hand shake as she placed a tea cup in the dishwasher. "Addison, finish telling us about your hiking adventure for this summer."

After the ladies left, Reagan retreated to her office to go over her schedule for the rest of the week. Wedding gown fittings, venue meetings, a bridal luncheon, and two possible new clients filled her week. She was ecstatic that the upcoming Saturday would be her first one off in a long while, but even more ecstatic that she was spending it with Blake and his family.

Now that she was alone, her thoughts trekked back to being in Blake's embrace once more. Last night had been like no other, and just thinking about it sent a shiver through her. She'd experienced tingling sensations that kept a huge smile on her face ever since he'd left that morning. However, Reagan couldn't help it. The man was amazing and downright knew what he was doing as if he was the founder, creator, and president in knowing how to please a woman. Every inch of her body had sizzled with pure ecstasy from his lips and hands. But it was more than just a lustful feeling she had for him and that scared her.

Her cell phone ringing bolted her out of her ardent thoughts and was slightly annoyed until she realized that it was her brother.

"Hey, Justin," she answered in a chipper tone, opening the lid of her laptop to turn it on.

"What's up, sis? Busy?"

Frowning, Reagan clicked the Internet icon with the mouse so she could check her email accounts. "Oh, no. Whenever you ask if I'm busy its important."

"Just received the test results and I'm a match."

"Wow! That's wonderful."

"Yes, and after talking it over with Shelbi and our father, I'm going to do the bone marrow transplant surgery with him."

"You know I'll be there to support you. When is it?"

"Not sure yet. He's meeting with the oncologist tomorrow. I just received the results this afternoon, but I'm sure as soon as possible. Within the next month or so. He's still taking the medication in the meantime."

"Let me know. I already told the girls I may have to take off for a bit so they'll be able to cover my events while I'm away."

"Perfect. I would love to have you there and I'm sure he would, as well."

Noting how Justin didn't refer to their father as Mr. Brown, she sincerely hoped that this would bring the two men closer together. Knowing her brother, he probably felt the same way.

After saying their good-byes, Reagan began to check and return emails pertaining to cakes, catering, and rental equipment. She'd been so engrossed in her work that she barely noticed when her intern assistant, Becca, walked in and placed a bouquet of red roses on the center of her round conference table.

"You have a special delivery, Ms. Reagan," Becca said in a sing-song tone as she slid the card from the holder and presented it to Reagan. "These are gorgeous. Do you need anything before I leave? I finished the party favor bags for the bridal luncheon, and made two hundred birdseed tulle pouches for the wedding next Saturday."

While Reagan heard Becca's ramblings, she barely comprehended as her eyes shot to the extravagant roses adorned with baby breath's and white tea roses scattered amongst what she assumed were two dozen red roses. They sat in a crystal vase with a red sash tied around the middle of it. Glancing down at the envelope in her hand, she saw that it was from Blake. She could sense hesitancy in her assistant as if she was dying to know who the flowers were from. Her wide eyes kept glancing at the card as she tried to purse a smile.

"Thank you for bringing in the flowers and making all the event favors. If you're finished for today, I'll see you tomorrow at nine sharp so we can set up for the luncheon."

"I'll be there."

"Perfect. Make sure to lock the front door on the way out. I'm not expecting any clients today."

Once Becca left and Reagan heard the chime of the alarm signaling the front door had opened and closed, she lifted the heavy bouquet and retreated to the sunroom. Placing the flowers on the coffee table, she plopped on the couch, hurriedly opened the envelope, and slid the card out. She was surprised and pleased to see that it wasn't typed but written in Blake's own handwriting. Luckily he wasn't a doctor who had messy handwriting, and she could actually read his neat cursive.

My dearest Reagan,

Last night was exquisite and I can't get you out of my mind, beautiful. I pray you're feeling better today and I hope that I'm the reason.

Yours truly,

Blake

Blushing over the last night part, she slid her cell phone from her dress pocket. Reagan figured she'd leave a message but was happy when he answered on the first ring.

"Hello, gorgeous. I was just thinking about you."

"Hey, Blake. Is this a good time?"

"Always a perfect time to speak with you. Actually, I'm at home resting. My afternoon was clear and since I barely had any sleep last night thanks to this fine sista I know, I decided to take a much needed nap before my five o'clock appointment."

"Your patients are lucky you're very accessible to them."

"It's a friend of my mother's. Of course I can't go into details, but she's like a second mother to me so I don't mind. Enough about that. How's my baby feeling today?"

"Much better now …. especially after the lovely roses arrived. Thank you so much. They brightened my day."

"My pleasure. I just wanted to cheer you up."

"Well, you certainly did."

"Great. For a moment I wasn't sure how you'd feel about last night considering your four month rule."

"We didn't break it even though it was quite tempting." She was almost upset that he'd brought up that damn rule. Goodness, she wanted to break it over and over and she knew after last night's tantalizing escapade with him that she would have no regrets.

"Yes, it was tempting. Too tempting. So if you need to slow down …"

Slow down? Heck, she wanted to speed up. "No … I'm fine, Blake. Let's just let whatever happens, happen in its own time."

"I will not argue with you on that. On another note, about this weekend's festivities. There's been a slight change of plans. Instead of chilling on my houseboat, we're going to use my parents' boat, The Lola. Its bigger and my father plans on grilling. He prefers his grill over mine."

"Sounds like fun."

"And you're going to try parasailing? I'm driving the speedboat."

The thought of being attached to a parachute high above the ocean while dragged by a speedboat made her nauseous. "Um … I'm still contemplating, but I will go jet skiing with you."

"Perfect. Can't wait either way. I don't care what we do as long as I see your fine bod in a bikini."

Heat rushed to her cheeks. He always knew what to say to make her weak at the knees. Now she had to go shopping to find a sexy new bikini and a cover-up considering it was a family outing. She couldn't be too sexy.

"You just concentrate on keeping me safe on the jet ski and the parasailing."

"So, that's a yes to the parasailing?"

"Mmm … only if you go really slow."

"I'll drive at whatever speed you can handle," he said in a low, deep voice. "Just scream out my name when you're comfortable and want me to go faster."

"You have a dirty mind, Doc." *Not that I care.*

"What?" he asked in an innocent manner. "That's your mind in the gutter. Just want to make sure you can handle the excitement and stamina of it all. It's a very … uh, thrilling adventure."

"I bet it is."

"Can't wait for you to find out."

"Are we still discussing parasailing?" she asked, crossing and uncrossing her legs. This conversation was causing her to have the urge to jump in the car and speed to his bed where he'd just finished his nap.

"Were we ever talking about parasailing?"

"You know what? I'm going to let you go."

"Alright, babe. Because if we keep talking like this best believe I will stop by after my appointment to finish what we started last night."

Stay strong, Reagan. "Hmm … on that note, I'm hanging up, but thank you again for the roses."

"I'll call you later."

She exhaled deep at the end of their flirtatious conversation. As tempting as it sounded, Reagan had to remain strong and not give into her naughty thoughts of being underneath him, enjoying just how slow or fast he wanted to go. After being ravished by his tongue as if he hadn't eaten in days, her curiosity was on high to any and everything else he could bestow upon her. Reagan had a feeling she would break her rule no matter how much willpower she thought she possessed, and for once she didn't care.

Chapter Ten

"Dad, the crab-stuffed salmon smells delicious," Blake complimented, holding out his plate as his father flipped the fish on the grill. "Feel free to throw one on my plate next to my infamous grilled steak and Parker's seafood pasta salad. I swear, baby sis put her foot in this." He picked up his fork and sampled a bite of the salad containing fresh shrimp, scallops, crab, and calamari.

"It will be done in a few minutes, son," the General stated in a baritone voice that was slightly deeper than Blake's. "Glad we decided to do this. Your mother loves when the entire family is here, and she is definitely happy about your new lady friend." He nodded his head in the direction of the two women who were on the opposite side of the top deck of The Lola making shrimp kabobs. "I guess things are serious between you two. I can't remember the last time you brought a girlfriend to a family outing. It's been a long while."

Blake glanced over to the beauty in question who was beaming bright and having a great conversation with his mother and sisters who now joined in after just jumping off the third floor deck into the ocean. Everyone had taken a liking to Reagan the moment they met her, just as he had.

"She's a special lady, Dad."

"Great to hear. Just want my children happy." He paused, placing the salmon on Blake's plate and gazing around the expansive deck. Leaning in toward his son, the General whispered, "I was just making sure the grandkids weren't around, but I see they're out on the speedboat."

"What's wrong?" Blake asked, concerned. The General was never one for being discreet around his family.

"Where is Cliff?" the General asked in a somewhat stern voice. "He's been missing in action for the past few outings and Parker keeps making excuses for him. Something isn't right."

Blake was glad that the jazz streaming through the speakers was loud enough so that Parker wasn't privy to the conversation. His dad trying to whisper was still somewhat loud. "You know married people. Perhaps they had an argument, or maybe he's really working on a project at work this weekend and couldn't make it."

"He's the senior engineer over a staff of twenty people. He should be able to delegate duties."

Blake wanted to laugh but decided against it as his father was not the joking type.

"Perhaps he's a micro manager. I'm sure if something was truly wrong Parker would tell us."

"I know when people are lying. I've intera—" Halting, he closed the lid of the grill and stared out onto the ocean in the direction of his grandchildren who were now preparing to water ski with his other son-in-law. "I know when people are lying to me, but most importantly, I've known my middle daughter for the past thirty-five years and her hesitation on a simple yes or no question tells me she's keeping something from us. Your mother is worried which affects me. I hate when your mother isn't happy."

Nodding, Blake thought back to the beginning of the week when Reagan was upset after the conversation with her father. While he was glad she finally got it off her chest, he hated hearing her cry. It had affected his heart in a way that he'd rather feel her pain just so she could smile again. Luckily, she'd been in better spirits the last few days and was traveling home to Memphis soon to be with her family during her father's bone marrow transplant. The thought of her being gone for at least a week did something to him he couldn't explain. Their connection had grown stronger with each passing day and being away from her had started to effect him.

He turned his head toward her direction only to find Reagan's radiant face on him. She was adorable in a pink and orange straw sun hat with a polka dot ban that matched the sarong wrapped around her cleavage area and stopped mid-knee. The urge to reach out and untie the knot to unravel all of the material to see her in the bikini spiked a nudge against his thin swim trunks. Remembering they weren't alone, he shook the provocative thoughts from his head and hoped he could make it through the rest of the afternoon without pulling her below deck. Perhaps if it was his houseboat, but he was on his parents' and they had cameras placed throughout.

After eating and resting his stomach for an hour, Blake was ready to take Reagan out in the ocean for some fun. Plus, he'd shared her with his family long enough and craved some one-on-one time. She'd eaten her lunch with the ladies on the middle deck while the men stayed up on the top deck manning the grills and watching golf on the flat screen.

"Hello, ladies," Blake greeted as he approached them. Reagan was lying comfortably on a double chaise lounge with his twelve-year old niece, Lana, who'd taken an immediate liking to her when they were introduced. They were busy studying something on Lana's iPad. "Can I steal Reagan away?"

"Noooooo, Uncle Blake. Ms. Reagan is showing me some books on the history of African kings and queens that I may be interested in. I just downloaded two."

Blake smiled at his niece whose favorite past time was reading and researching history. "That's wonderful, my little research worm. You can start reading one of them while we go jet skiing and tell me all about it when I return."

Rising, Reagan joined Blake. "Yes, I can't wait what to hear what you think about Cleopatra, Lana."

Blake and Reagan headed down to the dock where his two jet skis were waiting. His brother-in-law, Jerome, was already out on the water with his ten-year-old son, Jerry. Blake was still concerned about Parker and Cliff, especially when he'd noticed his sister wasn't wearing her wedding ring earlier. Of course it could be because they were on a boat outing, and she enjoyed diving off the top deck as well as jet skiing. When her cell phone rung earlier she frowned at it, huffed, but didn't answer it. He decided not to bother her at the moment and let her tell him when she was ready if indeed something was truly wrong.

Blake's gaze bounced back to Reagan who stood in front of him untying her sarong to expose a black bikini with pink orchids. The bottoms were more like boyshorts, which he didn't mind as they added more plumpness to her firm butt. Twisting her hair up on the top of her head, she took the scrunchie off of her wrist to secure it.

Reagan reached for one of the life jackets he held in his hands. "Are we going to share or ride together?" she asked, pulling on the life jacket as he did the same with his. "We can share if someone is using the other one."

Tapping his chin, Blake thought of about the perks of sharing one.

Giggling, she reached out and playfully punched him on the upper arm. "You're thinking dirty thoughts, aren't you?" She folded her arms across her chest.

"Yep," he answered nonchalantly, shrugging his shoulders. "You're fine as hell in your bikini."

"Thank you, and I must say I've enjoyed staring at your chest. Too bad the life jacket is going to cover it up but safety first."

Snatching her to him, Blake kissed her lightly on the lips but the touch of them were so succulent, he delved deeper into her mouth, showing no mercy. "I can take it off later on and anything else you want me to take off ... of yours." He kissed her once more as toe-curling sighs escaped her. The thought of her naked against his naked skin had aroused a passion in him that he wasn't familiar with. Reagan was everything he needed and desired—not just in a girlfriend but a best friend and a wife. He saw long-term, forever and a day with her. He saw always with her.

Laughing lightly, she pushed away and smiled up at him. "You know we're in public, right?" she asked, peering around the area that had other boats docked and families were out on the water just like his.

"Has it ever stopped us before? i.e. our first kiss?"

"No, but was your mother walking this way?" she questioned with a serious demeanor and straight face, nodding her head in the direction behind him.

"Please don't tell me my mother is behind me. She rarely gets off the boat."

"She's not." Reagan winked. "Just wanted to calm you down. You were hard as heck."

An arrogant grin reached across his face and he pulled her back toward him, relieved that his mother wasn't present. "Scared you may rip off my swim trunks, huh?"

"You're funny. You know what? I want my own jet ski. That way we can race."

"Hold up. As fun as that sounds, I always win against my sisters. I would hate to beat you."

A sly smirk rose up her left cheek, showcasing her cute dimple. "Not today."

114

"It's on, woman." While she was indeed a girlie girl, he loved the competitive, athletic side as well that he discovered a few days ago when she'd accompanied him on his morning jog. He thought perhaps he'd have to slow his pace—which he didn't mind—but was elated to see that Reagan could keep up with his regular speed just fine.

Prancing away from him, Reagan hopped on the light blue jet ski. She jerked her head over her shoulder and gazed at him with a seductive smile. "Changed your mind? You'd prefer to ride behind me, don't you?"

As tempting and taunting as that sounded, he followed suit and hopped on the purple one next to her. Leaning over for a kiss, she halted him by placing her hand over his lips.

"You are not going to distract me."

"Fine, but I'll let you have a head start, darling. After all, I am a gentleman."

"Not necessary. I told you I love to jet ski. Perhaps you need the head start, *darling.*"

"Alrighty then," he said, revving his engine. "It's on."

Revving her engine louder than his, she blew a kiss at him. "Bring it."

*****

Reagan couldn't believe all of the taunting she was doing with Blake, but she had to. The truth was, she didn't want to share a jet ski with him for the sheer fact that she didn't want to be next to him. Not in a mean, he stunk kind of way but more like she really, *really* wanted her body pressed against his, but she was trying to stay strong and focused. He had the freaking audacity to wear swim trunks and flimsy a T-shirt that did nothing to hide his smooth muscles underneath. She was relieved the shorts weren't flimsy, but when they'd kissed, she felt the immediate rise of his manhood as it pressed against her so hard she thought it would leap out of his trunks and maneuver itself between her bikini bottoms. In that instant, she'd yearned for him to make love to her right then and there. A voice

115

inside of her was screaming to tell him let's skip this family shindig and head on over to his houseboat which was docked less than a few blocks away. If they sprinted, they'd arrive there in five minutes, and she could be naked and really feel what had pressed against her inside of her.

Those ridiculous thoughts were what made her suggest that they ride separate jet skis and worse, race. That truly had to be the most ridiculous and outrageous thing that had ever passed her lips. Race? Sure, she'd race her girls a few times, but she never won as Addison was the most daring and competitive of them all. Nevertheless, here she sat listening as Blake's brother-in-law was in front of them on his jet ski going over how far out the buoys were and which way each of them should turn so they wouldn't crash.

"So, y'all good?" Jerome asked. "It's all in fun. I'd join in but you two look serious like there's a real prize." He paused, glancing back and forth at them. "Oh … well, hell maybe there is one. Me and my wife make sexy bets all the time. Anyway, I'll shoot the starter pistol off on the word 'Go'. Jr. and I will watch from the dock. Good luck and stay safe. Now shake hands or kiss. Or whatever." Laughing, he joined his son on the dock just as Lana plopped into an empty camp chair with her iPad.

Reagan turned her head toward Blake. He wore a calculating smirk and his eyebrows were raised to his hairline.

"Can a brotha have a little smooch?" he asked, leaning toward her.

This time she didn't stop him and kissed him lightly on the lips. "See you when you finally make it back, baby. I'll be sipping a margarita."

He snickered lightly and whispered, "Maybe we do need a bet."

"Mmm … okay. If … I mean when I win, you have to do a strip tease for me." *Why the hell did I suggest that? I really need my car washed and detailed, not more tempting moments with Blake.*

"Cool and *when* I win you *will* be doing a strip tease for me. Tonight."

They shook hands and got back into position on their jet skis. Reagan peered out to the third buoy that seemed so far away and really hoped she would win. She wasn't a great dancer and adding a strip tease to it would be even worse.

"Alright, you two," Jerome said in amusement as Jerry and Lana began to cheer loudly. He raised the starter pistol into the air. "On your mark, get ready, get set, and GO!"

They both zoomed off as the water sprayed up tall from the fast start. Reagan kept her eyes on the target even though she knew she was neck and neck with Blake who did give her a five-second head start. Her jet ski jumped up and down riding the water and she felt empowered and confident, especially when she passed the first buoy and made her way to the second. Blake got there first and she sped up faster as the machine's engine revved louder and bounced her up. Screaming at the top of her lungs she surpassed Blake to the third one, but when she made her turn around it to head back to the pier, he was turning at the same time. They briefly made eye contact and he winked at her before zooming off as water splashed on her. However, she wasn't discouraged as the idea of doing a strip tease tonight for him was out of the question. She caught up with him at the second buoy, passed him and blew a kiss at the same time.

Reagan wasn't out of the water yet as he caught up and ended up passing the first buoy at the same time which was designated as the finish line. They both slowed to a halt.

"Wait? Did we both just win?" she asked. "No, we have to do this again."

"Babe, I guess we both have the same determination and stamina. Good to know."

"Y'all racing again?" Jerome shouted out to them as they both rode up to the dock. "You gotta break the tie."

"Nah, bruh," Blake commented, reaching out and taking Reagan's hand in his. He kissed it tenderly and stared at her with loving eyes. "We're both winners, but I'll race you."

"Oh, it's on, man. I'll give you a few moments to rest."

Laughing at the two men as they started making their own bet of money, Reagan slid off of the jet ski and grabbed a towel to dry off. "I'll watch with Jerry and Lana."

Reagan loved the close-knitness of the Harrison family. While she was close to her brother and grandparents, there were times as a little girl that she wished it was Justin, her, and their parents living as one big happy family. However, she hoped one day that she would have the type of family she'd dreamt of as a child. Throughout the rest of the afternoon as she witnessed the Harrisons' loving interactions, Reagan realized that the only man she'd ever desired a family with was Blake. The newfound revelation plastered a smile on her face for the rest of the outing, and every time Blake beamed at her she had a feeling he could read her mind as his smile in return matched hers.

Chapter Eleven

"Blake, that was the best time I've had in a long while." Reagan plummeted on the chaise lounge on the top deck of his houseboat and reached out for the glass of wine he handed her. "Your family is so close-knit and fun."

Her breath stifled in her throat in awe over his bare, chiseled chest that had a golden hue thanks to being out in the sun all day. Now it was setting beyond the horizon in a beautiful array of vibrant orange, pink, and yellow tones. Blake had brought up a few candles instead of turning on the deck lights and it painted a romantic picture as she sipped her white wine.

He joined her on the edge of the chaise and raked a seductive gaze over her red bikini. She'd taken a shower when they'd arrived to his houseboat and changed into a sexy bikini for his eyes only.

"Yeah, we always have fun when we're together. Its hard with Clara and her family in DC, and with Parker and her crew even though she's an hour away, but her career and family keeps her busy."

"Your parents are so sweet and loving. I managed to speak with your dad in private again about the surprise vow renewal. He truly wants your mother happy. It's so sweet."

"Yeah, he may be some tough military general, but she's the only person who has him wrapped around her finger. Nothing he wouldn't do for her. Kinda like me with you. Nothing I wouldn't do to make you happy. I love when you smile, and I'm the reason."

She couldn't help but smile at his comment, and reached out to touch his face in a tender caress followed by a kiss on his cheek. "I see where you inherited it from. You and the General are a lot alike."

"I had a great role model watching my dad when I was growing up. I hope I can be a good husband and father like him someday."

Taking the last sip of her wine, she placed the empty glass on the table next to her. "I'm sure you will be." Something about the remark made her imagine him playing with their children or doing homework as she watched while whipping up dinner. Normally a thought like that would scare her, but with Blake it didn't. With Blake it was more of a welcomed reality.

He slid her down on the chaise until she was underneath him. "You think so?"

"Yes." Reagan could barely release the word before he settled his lips on hers in a slow, deep kiss. She encircled his waist with her legs, and he pulled her even closer to him. His bare chest against her skin was warm and sensual. She sighed out in relief for she'd wanted to yank him into a secret hiding place on his parents' yacht and kiss him but all the cameras put an end to her wicked thoughts. Now she was able to kiss him freely and tightened her grip around his body. She felt as though she wasn't close enough and meshed harder on him. His manhood was pressed firmly against her, and she wiggled her center to feel it even more.

"Alright, woman," he said, nibbling on her bottom lip. "Be careful what you ask for."

"Not asking. I'm telling you what I want."

"Mmm-hmm … and what is that?" A sly, arrogant grin raised up his jaw.

"You. All of you. Tonight."

"Then your wish is my command, my lady."

Blake kissed her again in the same slow rhythm as before, but this time each passing moment saw an increase of tempo, causing moans of delight to erupt from both of them. Reagan found herself engulfed in a passionate abyss of ecstasy and the anticipation of what was to come sent a fervent wave crashing through her. The intense desire she had for him since the second they'd met, finally escaped her as her heart opened up to the possibilities of forever with him. She didn't care about her four-month rule for the first time. She'd never craved a man as much as Blake, and while she was breaking her rule, she knew they'd be no regrets from her.

"You don't have anywhere to be in the morning, do you?" he asked, placing kisses along her neck.

"No. You?"

"Nope, which is perfect. I can take my time with you."

Blake untied her bikini top from around her neck, letting the straps fall. Sliding the material from under her back, he tossed it overboard. Her widened eyes at his gesture and Reagan giggled when she heard a splash.

"Oops. My bad, but you won't be needing it anyway."

"Apparently not. Now you have to make it up to me."

"With pleasure," he groaned.

Gliding his tongue in between her breasts, Blake teased along her skin, placing delicate kisses around her mounds that hardened with each touch of his lips. Sliding over to her right breast, he circled around the nipple before engulfing it in his mouth while massaging the other one. He continued driving her crazy as he wandered back and forth, causing tingles to shoot through her body and end in her center. Reagan didn't know how much more she could hold on without begging him to forget the foreplay, but at the same time she yearned to experience every moment of passion with him.

Lifting his head, Blake enclosed her mouth with his. Their wild, erotic tongue dance was an untamed chaos of passion as if they were already one, and she shuddered at the idea of actually becoming one with him. The electrical current that bolted through her veins sizzled and they were just kissing. She didn't know how much she could handle and this was only the beginning.

"I think we should take this below deck," she suggested when she heard people speaking nearby and rock music began to play.

"Oh, yeah. My neighbors are having a birthday party on their top deck tonight." Lifting off of her, he swooped her in his arms and carried her to the second floor landing. "Where to?" he asked.

She touched a finger to her chin. "Mmm … now if I remember correctly, you said we could make love all over your houseboat."

"That I did. However, I've pictured us together in my bed, so let's start there and see where we end up by the morning."

"Sounds like a plan."

Once they made it to his cabin, it was already lit with scented white candles everywhere. She was impressed with the romantic ambience and glad it wouldn't be dark. She wanted to see him the entire time they made love.

"You already had this planned," she said as he laid her on the sheets and followed on top of her.

"I saw the expression on your face earlier today."

"You know me well."

"I'm about to get to know you even better."

Blake's lips captured hers once again, this time more intense than ever before. At first she was taken aback and didn't know if she could keep up. Then she remembered he was *her* man and she met every stroke, every tongue loop, and every seductive moan with the same zeal he bestowed on her. The possessive and commanding way he kissed and caressed her, drowned her further into his realm of power that she craved more of. Never had a man made her feel loved, sensual, and a little naughty all at the same time. Blake had awakened all of her senses to be fully aware of the mind, heart, and soul connection that they shared. She was finally on a journey that she didn't want to end as she witnessed an amazing future with Blake flash before her eyes.

His hands traveled along her body until one of them ended at the top of her bikini bottoms. However, he wasn't moving fast enough in her opinion, so she reached down and eased herself out of them. He mouthed "thank you," and slid his hand over her center, massaging it in a counter-clockwise motion while their tongues mingled together in the same fashion. The fervor arising in her crashed through every cell in her body as she enjoyed the climatic feeling that was building up. She yearned for him to replace his finger with something else, and she pushed him off of her and flipped him over on his back.

"Well, damn, woman," He stared up at her with an amused smirk. "You have some strength."

"Only when I want something."

She pulled his swim trunks off to display what he had to offer, and her thoughts trekked back to the time when he told her he couldn't wear a regular sized condom. Now she saw with her own eyes exactly what he meant, and a warm, yet nervous as hell sensation rippled down her spine.

"Like what you see?" A cocky grin rose up his jawline.

"Oh, yes."

Chuckling, he slapped his hand playfully on her bare bottom. "Think you can handle it?"

"It's mine. So yes." *Goodness, I hope so.*

Reagan kissed him softly on the lips before sliding her tongue down his body until she reached her destination. Blake's groans turned her on even more as she stroked his length up and down while she enjoyed his amorous facial expressions. Replacing her hand with her tongue, sent a relieved sigh from him followed by an intense moan as she wrapped her lips around the tip of him and traveled her mouth downward. His hands weaved into her hair as she rose up and down on him in a smooth, unhurried manner. Her pace increased as his groans became louder which turned her on even more that he was satisfied by the job she performed. She gazed up at him and caught him reaching underneath his pillow. He pulled out what she figured he would and in one swift movement, she found herself back underneath him.

"I guess I'm not the only one with extra strength today," she teased, watching him secure himself and place her legs around his torso. "And I thought I was exhausted from being out on the water all day."

"Me too. But I guess we both have newfound strength from somewhere, and we'll need it … all night."

Blake entered her one inch at a time until he was nestled snug inside of her. A sweet moan released from her throat as she arched her head back against the pillow. Gripping his shoulders, she pushed her hips toward him as a hint to begin. His slow start was sensual and unhurried. Being one with him set Reagan's heart ablaze, and even though she knew it was too soon to be in love with Blake, she also knew that there hadn't been another man before him to make her feel complete.

Reagan wrapped her legs tighter around him as his thrusts sped up. He cupped her bottom tight, bringing her toward him over and over as their hips met each other's in a torrid, untamed way. Her moans grew louder along with saying his name over and over, and she hoped that the neighboring houseboat couldn't hear. She made out the faint sound of music from the party so hopefully her blissful screams of delight were drowned out because she couldn't remember a time when she'd been so noisy before. But there hadn't been a time when she'd been with a man who caused her to feel free to express herself however she needed to do.

"Blake ..."

"I love hearing you say my name."

"Mmm ... Blake ... you feel so wonderful, baby. Don't stop."

Lifting off of her, much to Reagan's dismay, he swooped her in his arms as she wondered where on earth they were going next as he carried her downstairs. However, she wasn't able to ask as his lips collided with hers in a strong, hard kiss. He ravished her lips like a tiger who hadn't eaten for days and was finally able to conquer its prey showing it no mercy. Placing her on her feet, his lips hadn't let up and she felt something cold on her back. Her eyes shot opened and she realized she was against the refrigerator. Reagan didn't want to admit to him she'd never had sex standing up before, and as he lifted one of her legs over his arm and plunged back into her, she hoped that she didn't fall over.

However, his strong hands clenched her hips as he delved into her, which held her steady. She grasped him tight around the neck as he hiked up her other leg and held her tight against him, bouncing her up and down as if she weighed next to nothing. He walked with her over to the couch, never missing a beat. She assumed he was going to sit down with her, but instead he continued standing in one place. An uncanny sensation rushed through her, causing her entire body to tremble, and a string of moans and curse words flew out of her as she exploded around him. It caused them to topple to the couch in laughter and she loved that not once did he stop even when he flipped her over.

Reagan sensed his climax near as his thrusts became longer and deeper. A series of heavy-breathing groans escaped him and he squeezed her tight, shuddering against her.

They made love two more times that night before falling asleep in each other's arms, sated.

*****

Blake kissed Reagan's forehead as she slept peacefully cuddled with the pillow he left in his place. He'd almost didn't want to wake her and preferred to stare at her for another hour. He'd spent one hour already watching her sleep while his thoughts jetted him back to last night. Making love to her was much more emotional for him than he'd expected. He knew he cared for her deeply, and while he'd toyed with the idea of her being the one, he now realized she was indeed the one. It hit him the second she'd stared up with her pretty brown eyes when he'd first entered her and she sighed out his name. Never had he felt so connected and at peace being with a woman. Blake was convinced that God created Reagan Richardson just for him, and he found himself falling faster than he'd anticipated.

He kissed her once more on the forehead and she stirred with a frown-type-of-a smile and yawned before opening her eyes.

"Good morning, beautiful."

"Mmm … good morning, handsome," she mumbled groggily. "I smell food. You cooked breakfast?"

"More like brunch. It's almost noon."

Sitting up, she stretched, propped up on her pillows with his help, and leaned back on them.

"Oh, wow." She rolled up the sleeves of his nightshirt she'd slept in. "We slept that long?"

"You did, but I wanted you to rest. You were worn out last night."

She stretched again with a long yawn. "Yeah, and my back is sore. I blame you … but no complaints."

"Glad I could be of service," he joked. "Now let's feed my baby."

He trekked to the food cart containing fried fish, grits, raisin toast, and scrambled eggs with cheese just the way she liked along with fresh ground coffee and orange juice. Removing the tray, he set it on her lap and rejoined her on the other side of the bed.

"Where's your food?" she asked with her fork midair with eggs.

"I ate while I cooked to make sure it was perfect for you since cooking is your hobby."

"Well, these eggs are delicious, Chef Harrison."

"Thank you." He swiped the remote from the bedside table and aimed it toward the television. "Anything you want to watch?"

"Not really. Do you have the music channels?"

"Yep. Which one?"

"Try one of the old school ones. Motown music."

He scrolled through the guide until he found what she'd suggested and the end of Marvin Gaye's "Let's Get it On" filled the speakers. They gave each other a knowing glance and he leaned over to kiss her cheek.

"Oh, this is my song," Reagan said, rocking to the beginning beat of "Knocks Me Off My Feet" by Stevie Wonder.

"Let's dance," he suggested, removing the tray from her lap and extending his hand to hers.

"Alright."

They danced around the bedroom laughing and holding each other while screaming the words of the song over Stevie at each other. He loved watching the sway of her hips and sparkle in her eyes when she was free and letting loose. Blake almost hated when the song ended and the next one didn't have the same feeling as a Stevie Wonder song. Pulling her into his arms, he dipped her and kissed her.

"So what do you want to do today?" he asked, lifting her back up but not releasing her.

"You," she said with a wink.

Chapter Twelve

"So I think if we use only a few calla lilies in each bouquet surrounded by roses you'll save money. Or you can have each bridesmaid carry three or four long-stemmed calla lilies tied with a bow to match their dresses," Reagan explained to a couple who was on a tight budget but the bride had over-the-top requests that caused the groom to cringe every time an estimated price was mentioned. Luckily, Reagan and Zaria were masters at creating elegant, classy, and over-the-top weddings on any budget.

Leaning across the table at Iguana Seafood Restaurant, Zaria patted the bride's hand as her face had grown solemn during the meeting every time the groom debated the prices. "The flower shop can send loose, long-stemmed lilies way less than me or them creating the bouquets. Then the hostesses can tie the bow around them the day of the wedding. I can show them. We've done it before with other flowers and its very elegant. Very cost effective."

The bride glanced at the groom who sat next to her in the booth, and her face perked up as the groom grinned and kissed her on the cheek.

"I like the idea, hon," the bride said. "And if we scratch the band and just have a DJ, I think everything will be fine. Right?"

"That will work," the groom answered. "I just want my sweetie happy."

Reagan smiled at the cute couple who were graduating from college in a few weeks and wanted to marry that July before moving to Atlanta soon after to start their lives.

"Yes, and so do we," Zaria began. "We don't want you to have any worries or stress. That's why we're here."

Reagan glanced at her cell phone as it vibrated on the table. It was a text message from Justin saying to call when she had a chance. She'd been worried about what was wrong during the entire meeting when he'd called earlier, left a voicemail, and then called twenty minutes later and left another voicemail. She rarely answered her personal calls when meeting with clients, but she was concerned as she hadn't heard either voicemail and now Justin was sending a text message. The last time he'd done something similar was a couple of years ago when their grandmother had died and Reagan was in the middle of a wedding rehearsal. He was the type not to state bad news in a text message and now she sat wondering what the hell could be wrong. She was due in Memphis soon for her father's bone marrow transplant, and now she feared the worst. Had something happened to him and it was too late?

Since Zaria had pretty much taken over, Reagan swiped the phone and excused herself outside of the restaurant. She didn't bother listening to the voicemails but instead called Justin immediately.

"Hey. I was with a client and haven't had a chance to hear your messages. What's wrong? Is Dad okay?"

Spotting an empty table at the back of the patio, she headed in its direction. The restaurant was dog friendly for outdoor dining patrons and she passed a few cute pups along the way.

"I figured you were in a meeting. Yes, he's fine. It's Shelbi. She's in the hospital."

Sitting down, she placed her hand over her heart as it sped up with anxiety. "Oh no. Is she okay? The baby?"

"They're both fine. Shelbi is calm now and we're going home soon, but she's going to have to be on bedrest and under close supervision for the rest of the pregnancy."

"What happened?"

"She started having pain and bright red blood. Raven says its placenta previa and it probably stems from the fact that Shelbi had a C-section with the last pregnancy. Luckily, she was at work at the practice when it happened and Raven had just returned from delivering a baby. Thank goodness my wife is always in good hands with a family full of doctors."

"Well, Raven is her sister and her Ob-Gyn so that is a blessing."

"I'm going to take some time off from the restaurant, which I was scheduled to do anyway with the bone marrow transplant. Now I'll be off longer but Derek pretty much runs the front of the house and my sous chef and other chefs can handle the kitchen."

"Don't worry about any of that. You just take care of your wife. I can come earlier if need be to help you."

"No. That's not an issue. You know her mother is already at the house setting up stuff and her sisters will be in and out as well."

"Of course. I'm not surprised. The Arringtons are a close-knit family, but I'm so sorry you have so much on your plate right now. I wish there was something more I could do."

"Just pray."

"Prayers already sent your way, big bro."

"I gotta go. The nurse is here to go over release instructions."

"Kiss Shelbi for me. Love you guys very much."

Later on that afternoon, Reagan sat cuddled with Blake on his lap in an Adirondack chair at the beach in front of her home. For the past month, they'd fallen into a routine of relaxing on the beach together whenever they had a chance. It seemed since they'd made love, they were finding ways to spend more time together without realizing that's what they were doing until her girls mentioned it.

She'd spoken to Justin again and Shelbi was resting comfortably with her mom and sisters by her side, yet Reagan could still hear the worry in his voice. She hated for her brother to have so much on his plate. Sighing, she snuggled closer to Blake's chest and gazed out to the ocean as the setting sun glistened on the water.

"Are you okay, babe?" Blake asked, kissing her forehead. "You've been very quiet."

"Just thinking about Justin and Shelbi."

"You'll be there next week if he needs anything."

"I know … I just hate being far away from Memphis sometimes. My brother is always so strong, but with Shelbi being on bedrest and then having to do the bone marrow transplant, he has to take it easy afterwards. I don't see him doing that."

"His hip will be sore for a few days from the withdrawal incision. He'll need to rest and not lift anything heavy for about a week."

"My brother isn't going to rest as long as Shelbi isn't feeling well, even with her family helping out. He adores her and dotes on her even when she's well."

"Yeah, but what can you do?"

"I can take the test to see if I'm a match so he can have one less issue to worry about. Now I regret not doing it when Justin did his, but once he said he was a match and was going to do it, I figured it would be a great way for him and our dad to be closer. That's something Justin has always wanted."

"Now I know why I love you," Blake stated sincerely. "We can have it done as soon as tomorrow morning."

"Um … that's fine." She tried to keep her tone even and steady but her chest had tightened and it had nothing to do with the test.

"Or right now if you really want to. It's just a simple blood test and cheek swab to test the HLA … I'm sorry, that means human leukocyte antigen to determine if you're a match."

Reagan already knew what HLA meant, but she was scared to speak because her tongue tied into a tight knot the moment he said the L word. He continued speaking but she'd managed to tune him out as the words *I love you* screamed loudly, blocking any other sounds. Blake had never said I love you before and she almost couldn't believe he meant them considering they hadn't been dating long. However, Reagan knew in her heart that he was sincere for it was obvious in the way he stared at her, spoke to her, and his actions toward her had already boasted it loud and clear. She'd just been in denial, but after their first passionate night together, she was aware that he'd fallen for her just as she'd fallen for him.

"So do you want to head to my practice now? Well … after you change out of your bikini."

His question jolted her out of her thoughts and back to the issue at hand. "Uh … sure. We can do it now. I have my dad's HLA marker results already. I asked him to send them to me just in case I decided to get tested with my primary doctor. I'll give them to you."

"Perfect. Let's go."

*****

Reagan had been quiet on the car ride to his practice, and while he was sure it was because of her brother and sister-in-law, Blake had an inkling that the fact he told her I love you may have also prompted her to quietness. He couldn't see her face when the words naturally slipped out because her head was resting on his chest, but her body had stiffened hard against his. Ever since, she'd managed to avoid eye contact and she was antsy. He wasn't upset she hadn't responded because he knew she was concerned at the moment about her family; though he was apprehensive that now he'd unleashed a white elephant in their midst. Blake didn't want her to feel obligated to say it back. In fact, he hadn't planned on telling her yet. He knew in his heart he'd fallen for Reagan the second he laid eyes on her and was on the road to falling in love since their first date.

"While you were taking a shower, I spoke to Jessica, one of my nurses who will meet us there. She's going to draw some blood and do the cheek swab. I also called your dad's doctor, Dr. Benson, but he was with a patient so I'm waiting to hear back from him. Luckily, Memphis is an hour behind so it's not quite 5 o'clock there. Hopefully he'll call me back today. Just wanted to give him ahead's up just in case."

Pulling into his parking space, he shut off the car and turned toward her. "Do you want to call your brother or your father to tell them?"

"No. I'll wait to see if I'm a match first. If not, I'll just stay in Memphis a little longer perhaps." She swiped her hands through her hair. "Maybe I'm rushing into this."

"No." Squeezing her hand, he brought it to her lips and kissed it. "You're being a good sister."

Smiling meekly, Reagan lowered her eyes and withdrew her hand.

She opened the passenger door and jumped out of the car before he had a chance to walk around to her side. Now he really knew what he said bothered her, but he couldn't and wouldn't take it back. He meant every word of it.

"Are you scared of needles?" he teased as they walked toward the building. He wanted to lighten the mood a tad. "Do I need to stay in the exam room and hold your hand?"

She twisted her lips into a smile and pinched his cheek. "No. I'll be fine, Dr. Harrison."

He was somewhat relieved that she finally perked up and the joking way she said his name. Maybe he'd jumped to conclusions, and she was nervous about being a match.

"Cool. I'll send your samples to the lab and more than likely to Dr. Benson to accurately compare with your father's. If you are a match you may have to do some more blood work when you get to Memphis ... that is if your brother even agrees to you doing this. I don't know him, but I have sisters. He's going to say no even if you're a match."

"Probably, but I'd feel better knowing that he wasn't stressed. How long will all this take?"

"I'm going to rush it so you'll hopefully know the day after tomorrow. Probably by the afternoon. Don't worry I've done this type of thing before," he teased with a wink as he opened the door to his office, turned off the alarm, and ushered for her to walk inside the waiting room.

"But of course. I guess I'm in good hands."

Pulling her toward him, he gazed at her tenderly. "You are in *very* good hands." He kissed her forehead and rocked them back and forth. "And about what I said—"

Placing a finger over his mouth, Reagan shook her head. "Don't worry about it. I know we were just having a casual conversation and it's something people say to each other. It's no biggie. We're cool. I know you didn't mean it in that way. We haven't been together that long."

Frowning, for that wasn't the direction he'd planned to steer the conversation, Blake was going to respond when the alarm chimed and Jessica strolled in still wearing her blue scrubs and a smiley face vest over the top. Reagan slipped out of his arms in a jiffy and smiled pleasantly at his head nurse.

"Hello, boss, and you must be Reagan." Jessica held out her hand and the women shook hands. "Nice to meet you. You can follow me to the exam room whenever you're ready."

"Thank you for coming back to work," Blake stated, opening the door from the lobby that led to the exam rooms and offices. "I appreciate it."

"No problem," Jessica answered, tying her blonde hair up in a ponytail. "Emergencies arise."

"I'll be in my office. Let me know when you're done, Jess."

Blake kissed Reagan on the cheek before heading back to his office with the nagging feeling that she knew she was lying to herself.

Chapter Thirteen

Two days later, Reagan sat at her desk staring at wedding dresses on her favorite boutique's website. She noted the ones her bride would probably like according to what she'd described, and those dresses would be pulled out before the bride and her mother arrived that afternoon. However, Reagan's eyes kept sneaking a peek at her cell phone as she contemplated whether or not to tell Justin she'd decided to see if her bone marrow was a match as well.

Sighing, she picked up the phone and pressed her brother's name in her contact list. She hated keeping anything from him.

"Hey, Reagan," he greeted. "Whatcha doing?"

She was glad he was in an upbeat mood, and she could hear the rattling of dishes in the background. "Just perusing wedding gowns."

"I'm assuming for a client."

"Definitely not for me." Even though she did see one she adored and saved it on her computer.

"I'm sure one day that will change."

Her thoughts soared back to when the words 'I love you' rolled off Blake's tongue so casually as if he told her that all the time. It had scared her to no end, and she could barely sleep last night as images of him repeating it filled her brain. Luckily, Blake didn't press the issue after she told him no biggie, but it was written on his face that it was a big deal. She had a notion he would bring it up again despite the fact she'd brushed it aside.

"Mmm, maybe one day. No time soon. How's Shelbi and the baby?"

"They're fine. She just ate breakfast and Raven is on her way over to check on her. Their mother spent the night and drove Jay to daycare this morning for me."

"And how are you?"

"I'm alright. I just hate that Shelbi has to be on bedrest. She's such a get-up-and-go type of person. At least this way she can finally rest before the baby arrives. The nursery is almost done. I just need to put the crib together."

"Her due date is still the same?"

"For now, but Raven is contemplating perhaps scheduling a C-section a week before the actual due date. She's monitoring them both for now."

"Well, I have something to share that may take some stress off of you."

"What's that?"

"I got tested to see if I'm a match for the bone marrow transplant. I'll know the results some time tomorrow."

"And why did you do that? I'm already doing the surgery. I start pre-surgery in a few days. Everything is set, sweetie."

"But if I'm a match then you won't have to. I can. With Shelbi on bedrest during that time, you'll have to take it easy as well. You'll be under anesthesia, which will make you groggy for a bit. Your hip will be sore for a week … you can't lift anything heavy during that time. What if Shelbi needs something? Plus—"

"Stop. Reagan, that is very sweet of you and I know you love me and Shelbi, but even if you are a match, I'm still doing it. You'll be here to help out and that's all that's matters."

"Justin—"

"No. I'm the big brother. End of conversation, Reagan."

I guess Blake was right.

Whenever her brother says 'end of conversation' with a little extra bass in his voice, he never changes his mind no matter how much she'd plead her case. She'd forgotten just how stubborn he could be at times.

"I wanted to help in some other way."

"I know. You've always had a kind and giving spirit like our mother. But honestly, I'm looking forward to the surgery in a way. I've been going with Dad to his doctor's appointments and we've bonded during this time. This will hopefully make our bond even stronger knowing he has my bone marrow. I thought you understood that."

"I do understand, Jay. I guess I thought you have so much on your plate with the restaurant, Shelbi, and little Jay's terrible two stage. Not to mention the barbeque sauce and spice lines, opening the second restaurant soon …"

"Sis, you know I have people in place for that. Right? I promise you everything will be fine. You're such a worry wart. Mom was like that. Now, I can't wait to see you next week and stop worrying. Okay?"

Knowing that was going to be impossible, Reagan sighed, but she did understand his position on the matter. "I'll try."

"I know you won't but everything is fine. I promise."

"Alright. And I'm staying a few extra days longer."

"That sounds wonderful. I appreciate that. I'm sure our father will as well. He has to stay in the hospital for a couple of weeks. Oh, and I met his lady friend yesterday at the restaurant."

"Oh really? Is she nice?"

"Mmm ... she's cool, I suppose. He's going to stay with her after he's released from the hospital for the rest of his recovery period. They seem kind of serious."

"Mmm ... well, that's good."

"So, speaking of significant others and getting serious. I spoke to Zaria. She says you may actually be in a relationship that will last longer than three months."

Thank you, Zaria.

"Um ... don't you need to go check on your wife?" She wasn't about to have this conversation with Justin.

"Nope. Raven just arrived, but I won't press the issue. I'll wait until I see you in person. You can tell me and Shelbi all about him while we're both on bedrest."

"We'll see. Now go check on your wife."

"Will do. And thank you for even considering taking my place if you're match. I'm not going to let you do it, but the thought means everything to me. Love you, baby sis."

"Love you, too."

After hanging up, Reagan read over her emails, but her jumbled thoughts kept clouding her brain. Mixed with barely no sleep for the past two nights yet wired thanks to two cups of coffee, her mind traveled back to the main reason she was dead tired.

Blake telling her he loved her just wouldn't shut off, and even though she'd brushed it aside with him, she had a notion he wanted to discuss it after they'd left his medical practice. However, he had an emergency with a patient and rushed off after dropping her off at home. Yesterday, she'd managed to stay busy all day with a client and only spoke to Blake once, but quickly cited she had to go but would call him back. She never did.

With her other boyfriends, Reagan never second-guessed herself with the relationship. Once she knew it wasn't going anywhere, she stopped dating them and never looked back. No point in wasting her time. And even when a few of them said the L word, it didn't scare her or make her nervous. Instead, it was more of a wakeup call with other men because she knew in her heart she didn't and never would love them back. It sure as hell didn't keep her up at night contemplating or questioning what she should do or if she'd made the right decision in breaking it off. But with Blake, Reagan was flattered and terrified all rolled into one. A complete first for her, and that scared her more than anything. Perhaps they were rushing. How could he possibly feel so strongly for her? Though deep in her heart and soul she knew he did. Blake wasn't the type of man to just say it. They'd already had sex ... no, made love, so he definitely wasn't trying to convince her to break her four-month rule because she'd already broken it with no regrets. Everything with him had been her first and the reality of that haunted her.

"Hey."

Reagan's eyes rose to see the object of her tossing and turning last night, as well as her current dilemma, leaning causally on the door jamb of her office. He was dressed in a pair of black slacks and a red golf shirt that showed off his delicious upper arm muscles. His five o'clock shadow gave him a distinguished, refined appearance yet at the same time she had an inkling he hadn't slept well either.

She shoved her thoughts to the back of her brain. "Hey, Blake. Surprised to see you."

"I was in the area and decided to stop by before heading back to the mainland."

"You want some coffee?" she asked, pointing her head in the direction of her Keurig.

"I can't stay long. Wanted to give you your results."

Her pulse raced with anticipation. "They're here?"

Blake nodded with a smile. "Yes, and you're a match, but ..."

"Wait, what?" she questioned, knowing she heard him correctly but she'd hoped she would be a match, as well.

"Yes, six out of eight HLA markers. Justin is seven out of eight. More than likely they're going to want to still go with him instead. It would be better for your father."

"Doesn't matter." She shrugged. "I told him I did the test and he said exactly what you said he would say."

"Not surprised. I'm a big brother, too. However, the fact that you wanted to relieve some stress from him says a lot about you. I admire that in you. Love that about you."

Her breath became caught in her throat and her heartbeat sped up faster than ever before. He said the L word again. It was in a different context considering he didn't exactly say 'I love you' yet it had the same effect on her. Little beads of sweat rested on her hairline and the back flips in her stomach made her nauseous.

What the heck is wrong with me?

Rubbing the back of her neck, Reagan placed a pleasant smile on her face and summoned up all her strength to brush it off in order to continue the conversation.

"You were right," she started, darting her eyes away from his and scrolling through her emails even though they were blurry as she tried to concentrate on speaking without stumbling over her words. "Must be an overprotective brother thing. Plus, in a way I'm happy that its Justin. He's wanted to be close to our father for as long as I can remember. This has been a good bonding experience for them, and now that I've told my father how I feel, I'm able to move on without despising him anymore."

"Mmm-hmm," Blake said, nodding his head as he rested his hand on his chin and tapped it with a finger. "I see. That's good."

"I guess it all worked out. I've decided I'm going to stay a little longer. Two weeks instead of one, but I'll be back in time for your parents' wedding anniversary celebration. Everything is pretty much set, and Zaria will be here if need be for your mom."

"Reagan, you know I'm a doctor. Right?"

Frowning, her brow wrinkled at his questioning. "I appreciate you helping me through this. Do I need to give you my insurance card or something for the test?"

Stepping all the way into her office, he shoved his hands in his pocket. "No. That's not what I meant."

"What do you mean?" she asked, confused by his demeanor.

"Your face is flushed and you're hot. You keep lifting your hair and rubbing your neck. It all started when I said the word love. Your facial expression was priceless. At least this time I'm able to see it as I said it."

Oh great. I was trying to avoid this. "No. No. No. That doesn't bother me. It's … not like you mean it … in that way." She laughed nervously but his expression was stuck on serious.

"Doesn't bother you? I beg to differ. You've been ignoring me since I said it. You clearly brushed it aside the other evening, but I didn't say it in a casual manner. Yes, it naturally slipped out. Shoot, it scared me too in a way, but I was telling you the truth. I love you, Reagan. Very much. I wasn't waiting for a response and I'm still not. Before you leave for Memphis, I want you to know that I do love you."

"Oh …" Reagan stopped as she thought about the times she'd heard the same words from other men and it meant absolutely nothing and had no effect whatsoever. This time was different. This time her heart hammered so hard against her chest she was positive he could see it pulsing through her blouse.

"Blake, I just think it's a little early in our relationship to throw around the L word."

"Throw around? Reagan, I wouldn't have said it if I didn't mean it. I fell for you the second I laid eyes on you. I knew you were the one."

"It's just too soon for me."

"I know about your fear of commitment and relationships. I know where it stems from. Just think about

142

us while you're gone, and we can talk about our relationship when you return. The important thing for you right now is supporting your family, and I respect that."

"I think me being away for a few weeks will be good for us. Taking a break will be a good idea." Even as she said the words her heart cringed. *What the heck is wrong with me?*

"Break? I didn't say break. I still want to talk and text you everyday."

"I know you didn't. I'm saying it."

His face scrunched into a ball of perplexity. "Oh, wow. I see. So you're going this route again?"

Standing, she crossed her arms over her chest. "I beg your pardon?" Her voice rose louder than she'd intended. Brooklyn's office was next door, but Reagan wasn't sure if her best friend was in there or not as she preferred to work outside on the veranda at times.

"You break up with men when you feel threatened with a long-term commitment because of your parents. You're scared of what may happen, and I understand that, but I'm not your father, Reagan. I wouldn't leave you for anything in the world. I know what I want and I know what I have in you. I'm not going anywhere. Wild horses can't drag me from you. So if you want to take your little break and not talk to me while you're away from me to realize that, then do it. I'll be right here when you return. Still in love with you."

"It's just …" She halted as the emotions welled in her. "Blake, I can't explain it. I just know whenever you say it I get jittery, but the thought of being without you breaks my heart into a gazillion pieces. It's … I don't know how to explain it. I'm having a lot of firsts with you."

Darting to her side, he pulled her to him. "I'm not going to rush you, Reagan. I'm not asking you to marry me tomorrow. While I'm not happy with the break, I'm not the type of man to give up … especially when I know what I want. But I will give you some time."

Candace Shaw

"I appreciate that."

"I really hate to leave right now," he said as his jawline clenched, "but I have a patient in an hour at my practice."

"No problem. Thank you for telling me the results and for understanding."

He slid his hands off of Reagan, pivoted toward the door, and closed it. Making his way back to her, Blake scooped her in his arms and imprisoned her lips with his in a ravishing, mind-blowing kiss that nearly knocked her over. However, he held her tight against his body as the hungry kisses continued. The emotions cascading over her were like no other time in her life. They went from rapturous to pleasure to terrified to a sense of an awareness that resonated a tranquil peace within her heart and soul. Here was the man that loved her, and thus far had done everything to show her not just tell her.

His possessive kisses intensified and she welcomed the passionate way he always made her feel as if she was the only woman in the world to him. She felt the same and couldn't even imagine another man ever touching or kissing her the way Blake did. It was as if he was truly created just for her. So why was she nervous and scared straight every time he said I love you? Yes, she could admit that her daddy issues had been a hindrance in past relationships, but at the same time no other man made her heart flutter with delight every time he walked into a room.

Blake lifted her up on the desk, placing her legs around his waist. She was in a state of bliss and barely realized when he removed his hands from her body but not his lips as they seduced her neck with a blazing tongue.

"Mmm ... Blake, you feel so good."

"Tell me something I don't know," he groaned against her neck. He unzipped his pants and proceeded to yank up her dress and panties down with his free hand.

Her right leg began to shake uncontrollably with anticipation. "You are so wrong for this."

"What?" he asked, rotating his tongue with hers in an untamed, overzealous way. "Making love to my woman before I leave? Not to sound like a possessive prick, but you're mine. All mine. I just want to remind you."

Tingles shot across her skin and landed in a puddle of scorching heat in her center. The thought of being all Blake's presented an uncanny rush of adrenaline to jolt her heart into surrender for she'd never truly felt a sense of belonging or feeling needed by a man before.

Out of the corner of her eye, she saw him toss a gold foil wrapper on the floor and a devilish smile crossed his face as he slid into her with one long stroke.

"Mmm ... yes, Blake ... my goodness," she screamed out, gripping his shoulders tight as he thrust in and out in a sensual, deep rhythm. Her ardent moans increased when he clenched her bottom and guided her to him. She relaxed her head back as he dropped scorching kisses on the top of her breasts and up to her neck back and forth in a manner that matched the figure eight rotation of her hips. Her pleasure moans echoed through the office and then stopped as she remembered something.

Placing her finger over her mouth, Reagan nodded her head toward the wall on the right. "Shhh. I think Brook is next door."

He chuckled sarcastically. "Then you better be quiet," he whispered against her lips, thrusting even deeper inside of her. "That is, if you can."

A wicked grin slid over her face. "I'm not the only one," Reagan said, crashing her mouth on his and gyrating her hips hard against him. The mere touch of him on her skin always sent her over the edge, but she'd realized the last time they'd made love, she had the same issue.

She almost laughed out loud at Blake's exaggerated facial expression as he tried to keep quiet and in control. However, she sensed his climax was near as he clutched her hard against him and carried her to a chair on the opposite wall, never missing a beat. He sat down with her on top of him, pulling her up and pushing her back down over and over until her entire body shuddered in pleasurable agony. She just knew she'd have fingerprints etched into her bottom from how hard he'd clenched her skin because 1) to keep himself from making a sound and 2) to drive her completely insane … as he was doing, and she enjoyed every amorous moment of it.

Reagan buried her head in his chest to muffle the ardent sounds she desperately needed to scream out and squeezed his upper arm biceps tight to restrain herself. His hands continued to grasp her butt as he never stopped the pace of their feral tempo. She didn't know how much more shooting sensations she could handle without calling out his name.

"I see you're trying your damnedest not to say anything, babe," he teased, lifting her off of him and repositioning her in the chair so that she was on all fours in it. He stood behind her and leaned over, lifted up her hair, and placed a sensual kiss on the back of her neck as his grip tightened on her mane.

Reagan's breath stifled in her throat as he continued laying sweet, erotic kisses on her neck while he weaved his hand throughout her curls.

"You sure you want a break from me?" he asked, popping her bottom playfully and sliding all the way inside of her.

She glanced at him over her shoulder. "You would have to ask like that, huh?"

"Just checking," he replied, sliding all the way out and back again in one single, fluid motion as his tongue roamed along her skin. "I know you're going to miss me."

Blake continued in an unhurried pace as she met his sensual thrusts over and over. The emotions charging through her body were weakening any resistance of the break she'd mentioned earlier. She didn't even know why she'd suggested it for that was never the plan. He had a way of making her feel needed. Special. Loved.

He rested his forehead against the back of her head as his breathing and movements began to unravel. Wrapping his arms tight around her waist, Blake shuddered uncontrollably. Turning her head slightly to his, Reagan kissed him to smother any sound or curse words he probably needed to shout out.

Once he calmed down a bit, he eased out of her. "Goodness, I hate leaving you," he said, helping her up.

She slammed sated back into the chair. "I know, but duty calls."

"Be right back." He disappeared through her door that led to her bedroom from her office.

She pulled down her dress and took three quick strides to her desk to check her security monitor on her cell phone.

"Whew." Reagan ran her hand through her messy hair and plopped into her chair with a nervous giggle. "Brook is on the terrace and not in her office."

Later on that night, she lay nestled in Blake's arms after a long lovemaking session because the ten minute quickie wasn't enough. Her mind raced with what ifs and was she doing the right thing about taking a break while she was away. The idea of not communicating those two weeks seemed like a good idea when she thought of it, but saying it out loud didn't make any sense to her. Plus, his question of 'are you sure you want a break from me?' had played in her head all day after he'd left. For the first time in her dating life, she was at a point of realizing she was finally falling in love with the man of her dreams.

Chapter Fourteen

"Girl, I'm so happy you're here with us," Shelbi Arrington-Richardson said, rubbing her belly tenderly. "You've been such a sweetheart taking care of us these last few days." She glanced over at her husband who was lying next to her in the bed as he dozed in and out while he attempted to watch his best friend, Rasheed Vincent, at a press conference about buying a stake in one of the top NBA teams. Justin still had some pain in his hip from the bone marrow retrieval location and had finally taken Reagan's advice to rest. Plus, the pain medication that he didn't want to take made him drowsy.

"That's why I'm here," Reagan replied from her spot on the loveseat in the sitting area of Shelbi and Justin's downstairs guestroom. Since Shelbi was instructed to avoid stairs while on bedrest, the couple opted to sleep in the guestroom with Shelbi sometimes retreating to the couch in the family room for a break from the bed.

"Well, we appreciate it. Between my parents taking Jay Jr. for the week, my siblings, and you spoiling us with this delicious breakfast and last night's dinner, I could almost get used to this ... except I hate being on bedrest." Shelbi exhaled and it ended in a pout. "I can't even go up to the nursery anymore."

"I know, sweetie, but you'll meet your little princess, soon."

Shelbi beamed with delight once more as she rubbed her belly again. "I can't wait. Thank you for all the adorable clothes for the baby. She's going to be the best dressed baby girl in Memphis."

Walking over to the bed, Reagan grabbed the trays from breakfast and sat them on the table in front of the couch. "No problem. Hopefully it will make up for not being here for your baby shower, but it's the weekend of the Harrison's anniversary dinner."

"I completely understand. Those are Blake's parents. And speaking of ..." Shelbi's eyebrows rose while a grin settled on her face.

"Blake is fine," Reagan answered, settling back on the couch. "I spoke to him briefly while I cooked breakfast. I had a question about his parents' event." *And I needed an excuse to call him.*

"I love how you glow whenever he's mentioned. In fact, you've been glowing since you arrived. He must be the one, and I can't wait to meet the man that finally has my sis in love."

Heat rose to Reagan's cheeks at the prospect of finally being in love. She knew in her heart that she loved Blake, and denying it any longer was out of the question. Especially considering everyone around her could see it plastered on her face—including him more than likely. The thought of introducing Blake to her family seemed like the natural thing to do. She'd never considered it with some of her other boyfriends because the relationships weren't ever serious for her.

"So you spoke to him this morning? I could've sworn you said you were on a break and weren't going to speak to him. I think someone is missing someone and my bet is it's you."

Reagan had somewhat ignored her alleged break idea because she'd missed Blake more than she cared to admit. She'd called him first to say she'd made it safely to Memphis. It was as soon as the airplane had landed and was seated on the runway waiting to advance to the gate. She'd begun to miss him as soon as he'd dropped her off at the airport and every time she'd thought about not being in contact for two weeks felt like it would last an eternity.

"I didn't break up with him before I left, but … it's all moving so fast for me. He's in love with me, and for the first time it doesn't bother me to hear a man tell me that. Instead, it bothers me that it doesn't bother me and so in a way it bothers me. Does that even make any damn sense?"

"It does actually," Dr. Sean Arrington stated in a serious manner.

Reagan pivoted her head to see Shelbi's big brother standing in the doorway wearing a dark blue suit, red tie, and a pleasant smile across his handsome chocolate face.

"Well, please explain it to me. I could use a professional opinion."

"For the first time, you finally feel the same way back, and I can understand from personal experience how that feels. Now I have no idea what the entire situation is, but as a psychiatrist, just hearing the last part of your conversation conveys to me that you're in love and it scares you because of your dad's abandonment of you and Justin at a young age. It's affected your relationship with men over the years. You had a pattern and now its broken. It's only scary because it's something you've never had to deal with before. It's a new experience and you're trying to put everything into perspective. But that's just my opinion."

Reagan listened to Sean who was usually a jokester; however, he never joked about his analysis for his patients or giving advice to family. "Wow, Sean. Thank you. I know you're right. It's a little scary, and yet I can't stop thinking about him. He's been respectful of my break idea.

150

I'm the one that has called him three times and texted once since I've been here for almost a week. He hasn't initiated anything or brought up our relationship which is making me miss him even more."

Shelbi clapped, causing Justin to open his eyes and glance back and forth at everyone. "I had a crazy dream that my baby sister is actually in love."

"Yes, dear. Go back to sleep." Shelbi kissed his forehead as he dozed off on her shoulder. "Sean, you showed up just in time because her rambling did confuse me for a moment."

"Are you going to send me a bill?" Reagan asked.

"Nah." Chuckling, Sean strolled into the room and hugged Reagan. "It's on the house. This time," he teased with a wink. "I went to Meharry with Blake. He's a good guy, and if he told you he loves you, he meant it. I remember when Garrett and I were busy chasing skirts in our free time, Blake would be in the library studying. He's always been focused on his career and opening a practice after med school. Everything else was secondary, so if he's finally found the one, I'm happy it's you."

"Well, thank you, Sean. I'm going to let you hang with your sister for a bit. I have to make a phone call," Reagan said, grabbing the breakfast trays and heading to the door.

"You're going to tell him now?" Shelbi asked in a chipper tone. "I'm so excited."

"No. I'll wait until I see him again in person to tell him. I have a conference call with a bride in about ten minutes and then off to the hospital to see my dad."

"Send him our love. Hopefully Justin will be able to go with you tomorrow."

After her conference call, Reagan headed to the hospital to visit her father. He was four days status-post the bone marrow transplant, and would have to stay in the hospital for at least two weeks to monitor his progress. When she arrived, the nurse at the desk gave her scrubs, gloves, a hair bonnet, and a face mask to wear to prevent her father from any infections as his immune system was low at the moment. This was her third visit since the surgery. Because he was in a special bone marrow transplant center, visitations had been limited to two people at a time. His girlfriend, Rhonda, was there for majority of the time.

After changing into her scrubs, Reagan stuffed her sundress into her tote bag and proceeded to her father's room just as his doctor was exiting.

"Hello, Ms. Richardson." Dr. Benson glanced up from the tablet in his hand. "Came to check on your pops?"

"Yes. How is he feeling today?"

"We were finally able to remove the feeding tube this morning, and he had a very light breakfast. Each day is a process of him getting stronger. Glad you're here. Rhonda just left but should be back in a few hours."

"Who else is here?"

"Just you."

"Okay. Thank you."

Reagan realized this would be the first time she would be alone with her father since she'd arrived in Memphis. Justin, Rhonda, or one of her father's friends had always been present. Breathing in, she pushed the ajar door open and peeked her head inside. Her father was propped up against the pillows watching television and sipping water through a straw.

"Dad?" She stepped into the room to make her presence known.

Giving a weak smile, he motioned for her to come in. "Hey, baby girl." His voice was groggy but his expression perked up when she entered. "Glad to see you."

He reminded her of Justin that morning as he lay in bed half sleep watching television. Both men had the same light brown complexion, curly hair, facial structure, and medium build. It was as if their dad had spit Justin out except their personalities. Justin would never desert his family.

Reagan headed toward her father and gave him a hug, being careful not to touch the IV in his lower arm, then settled in the chair next to the bed. She glanced up at the flat screen to a story on Rasheed Vincent on the Sports Channel.

"I'm sure Brooklyn is also watching her brother's new accomplishment," Reagan stated.

"I remember when he was a skinny little kid playing street basketball with Justin. Now he's part owner of a basketball team. I know his parents would've been proud of him, and of Brooklyn, too."

Reagan nodded. Her parents and the Vincents had all grown up together in the same neighborhood in Frazier, an area in Memphis. Mrs. Vincent had lost her battle with breast cancer, and her husband had died a year later from a heart attack. Brooklyn was a senior in high school upon her father's death, and Rasheed became her legal guardian. Reagan's grandmother had always stated she sensed that Mr. Vincent had died of a broken heart because he missed his wife. They'd always been a sweet, loving couple and Reagan had enjoyed chatting with Mrs. Vincent because she'd been best friends with her own mother and would tell stories about their lives growing up.

"I'm sure they would have been."

"They're smiling down just like your mother and grandparents are for you and Justin. You two make me proud as well. You both own successful businesses and Justin is a great husband and provider. I know I wasn't a great dad like I should've been, but I love you and I appreciate the two of you more than you could ever realize."

"We know, Dad. I'm just glad we have another chance to be with you." It felt weird calling him Dad in person, but she'd started to get used to it and enjoyed the little twinkle in his eye when she said it.

"Death was definitely knocking at my door, but I've been given a second chance at life thanks to my son. I just hope that the two of you will give me a second chance to be in your lives. I know I messed up in the past, but now I don't want to miss anything."

"And you won't … but let's not worry about that now. The most important thing at the moment is you regaining your strength and building your immune system back up."

"You know, Justin told me you were tested and are a match as well. I thought after our conversation, you probably didn't care to find out."

Reaching out, she grabbed his hand and held onto it tight. "Honestly, at first it was for Justin because of Shelbi being on bedrest, but once I found out I was a match, an inner peace prevailed, and it reminded me that I'm your daughter and that I have a parent who is still alive. I intend to make every effort to be a presence in your life."

"That means a lot to me, and I promise to meet you halfway … no, all the way."

"As soon as you're well enough, you and Ms. Rhonda should come to St. Simons Island for a visit. It's a very relaxing beach city, even during the busy season."

"That's a great idea. We'd love to come, and will I meet this young man of yours?"

"Yes, I'd love to introduce you to Blake."

"Ah, so is he the one?"

"You know, Dad, for the first time in my life I can say yes to that question."

"Mmm … that's good to know."

Reagan watched him doze off to sleep and was glad that they'd had a chance to speak without others around. For once she was able to talk to her father without being nervous or have the feeling of not being loved by him. She knew he felt guilty, and in a way she felt guilty as well and hated that it took for him to almost die to realize she needed to also make the effort.

Chapter Fifteen

"Your golf game sucks today, Blake, and I'm loving every minute of it," Garrett said as he watched Blake's ball soar through the air only to bypass the tenth hole and land in the pond with a splash. "You keep this up and I'll have enough money to pay off my new Benz."

Wrinkling his brow, Blake slid his club back in the bag and headed toward the golf cart. "You don't have a new Benz." He set the bag in the back and hopped in the passenger seat as Garrett drove to the eleventh hole.

"Nope, but at $25.00 over par, I will. Man, seriously what is up?"

Grabbing his water bottle from the cup holder, Blake gulped a long swig, wishing it was something stronger. He didn't really want to confide in his friend that he missed Reagan and it had affected every part of his life. It had been a week since she'd left for Memphis and he'd only spoken to her a few times about her father's progress but nothing pertaining to their relationship. Trying to give her the break she asked for hadn't been easy. Dropping her off at the airport and watching her walk away had twisted his heart into a double knot. Over the last week it had tightened to the point of swearing he was having a heart attack. He feared history would repeat itself and she would return to St. Simons but not to him. He was in love with Reagan and the thought of losing her wasn't an option.

Sighing, Blake shifted in his seat. "Nothing, G."

"Mmm-hmm. You know I've been in your shoes before, right? Those Richardson women are something else."

"Tell me about it. I told Reagan I loved her, and the wall that I thought I'd bulldozed down shot right back up."

"I heard. You know, my wife has been low-key planning y'all wedding. The good thing is Reagan didn't dump you. That's her usual pattern."

"No, but she did ask for a break. I've been respectful of it but …"

Garrett glanced over at his friend with an amused smirk. "It's causing you to not shave, lose golf games, and actually confide in me."

Blake rubbed his five o'clock shadow and jumped out of the golf cart as Garrett came to a halt. "Something like that. At least work has me occupied. But once I'm alone all I can think about is her and restraining myself from jumping on the next flight to Memphis."

Garrett trekked to his bag and pulled out a golf club along with a ball from his pocket. "You got it bad."Strolling over to the tee, he set the ball down on it. "Well if you decide to go to Memphis, let me know. Dr. Felix and I will handle your patients."

"I was joking." *Wait. Am I?*

Garrett peered over his shoulder at Blake while taking a few practice swings. "Joking? You sound pretty serious to me."

Blake didn't answer but remained silent as Garrett concentrated on his swing. The truth was in a way he wasn't joking. He wanted to rush to the airport at that moment and take the next flight out. Reagan was the kind of woman who desired more than to just be told I love you. She needed action, considering growing up her father may have told her he loved her but never showed it. Even though she'd made up with her father, Blake sensed that her heart wouldn't fully heal until she knew that the man who loved her would do more than just say it.

"So you and Dr. Felix can handle my patients for a few days?"

"No new Benz for me." Garrett stopped mid swing, turned toward the golf cart, and slid his club back in the bag. Taking his cell phone out of his pocket, he began typing. "You take the wheel while I search for the next flight to Memphis."

*****

"Raven, I'm so glad you dragged me out of the house tonight." Taking a sip of her margarita, Reagan perused her brother's crowded dinner and blues club, which was named after their mother, Lillian. "It has been a long week, so cheers to you." Raising her glass in the air, she clinked Raven's glass and both ladies took a sip of their drinks.

Raven pushed her reddish-brown, natural curls behind her ears. "After delivering three babies back to back and an emergency C-section, I needed tonight, too."

"Another toast to you for bringing life into this world." Reagan raised her glass again as Raven clinked it and the ladies downed their drinks followed by silly laughing.

Lifting the pitcher of frozen margarita from the table, Raven refilled their glasses. Reagan almost refused but then remembered Justin lived on the trolley route by the river, and she didn't have to drive. Raven's husband dropped her off and was picking her back up in a few hours so she could enjoy herself.

"You know, I'm glad you and Justin are close with your dad now. I hate that it takes people to have near-death, or some other tragic experience to realize what is truly important, and now your father knows he missed out on so much."

Reagan nodded as she reminisced on earlier that day when she and Justin had visited their father. They'd watched home movies of Justin's wedding and other special occasions their father had missed. "Me too. My grandmother used to say better late than never, and I'm looking forward to spending time with him."

The waitress dropped off their appetizers of spinach dip, fried calamari, and chicken wings with Justin's Tangy Brownsugar Barbeque Sauce. As the ladies began to eat while listening to the blues band, Reagan's thoughts trekked to Blake and how much she missed him. Upon entering the restaurant, a handsome gentleman asked her out, another one asked her to dance, and a third one offered to send drinks. Normally, she'd at least be cordial to any man who approached her, but since being with Blake and realizing she loved him, no one else had piqued her interests.

The vibrating of her cell phone on the table caught her eye, and she halfway hoped it was Blake, but Zaria's picture from her wedding day graced the screen.

"Hey, cuz," Zaria greeted in an abnormally loud yet peppy voice. "Whatcha doing?"

"Hey, Z. Just chilling with Raven at Lillian's."

"Oh ... cool. Chilling with Raven at Lillian's. Cool."

"Why are you so loud?"

"Um ... I figured you couldn't hear me because of the band. Which one is playing tonight?"

"Raging Bulls."

"Love them. I booked them ages ago to play there. Glad they're still regulars. So ... did you just get there?"

"Yep. About twenty minutes ago."

"Mmm ... okay. Where ya'll headed next?"

"Home probably." Reagan frowned at her cousin's odd questions and loud tone.

"Well, have fun and stay for awhile. You deserve some relaxation."

"We have a VIP booth for three hours. I think that's long enough."

"Yes! Three hours is good. Okay, girl. Tell Rave hello for me. Bye."

"B—" Reagan could barely say bye before Zaria hung up. "That was Z. She said hello."

"How is she?" Raven inquired, dipping a calamari into the marinara sauce.

Reagan rubbed her ear. "Fine I guess. Odd conversation. My eardrums are ringing and it's not from the band."

For the next hour, they ate and danced together before settling back in the booth when the Raging Bulls took a break and the DJ began to play B.B. King songs.

Raven's cell phone lit up in the middle of the table, and she slid it toward her as her eyes and smile widened. "Oh." She glanced up at Reagan and back at the phone screen while rapidly typing.

"Must be your hubby."

"Yeah, girl … he's flirting with me."

The music suddenly stopped and everyone's attention shifted to the DJ booth. "Alright, now grown and sexy people. This is DJ Silky Smoove, and I just received a special request from a gentleman who's so in love he hopped on a plane to surprise his lady. This song goes out to her. He said as soon as she hears it, she'll know it's from him and should start wondering whether or not he's in the building."

"Ah … isn't that sweet," Reagan said, sipping her water to cool down from dancing. "He must really love her."

"Isn't it though?" Raven picked her cell phone back up and commenced to typing once more. "She must be the one."

The song began and Stevie Wonder's voice sounded through the speakers singing the first verse from "Knocks Me Off My Feet." Reagan rocked back and forth with a slight giggle as she glanced around to see who else in the building had the same favorite song as her. Some couples headed out to the dance floor, but most of them she recognized from dancing earlier. She didn't see any couples rushing to each other and kissing madly.

Reagan decided to ignore the rapid beat of her heart, the goosebumps that tickled over her skin, and the silly notion that the song was for her. Yet her eyes couldn't help but scan the dance floor, and Zaria's weird phone call only heightened her curiosity. She glanced at Raven—who was usually cool under pressure and the most level-headed of the Arrington siblings—trying to keep her lips from exploding into a smile and her eye contact elsewhere.

Reagan felt herself rise from her seat as if in an out-of-body experience and float toward the entrance where the lobby and restaurant met. The margaritas had finally kicked in and were apparently causing hallucinations because the handsome man headed toward her wore the same amazing smile as Blake.

"Hi there," he said. "You're stunning in my favorite blue dress."

Feeling the emotions soar through her body and happy-tears well in her eyes, Reagan ran and jumped straight into his arms. "I love you. I love you. I love you, Blake," she repeated over and over while laughing and placing kisses all over his face, not realizing the hard force she'd used to jump up on him had caused them to tumble to the floor all at the same time.

Normally she'd be embarrassed yet Reagan didn't care as patrons watched and clapped. She saw Raven's shoes out of the corner of her eye and realized she was in on the surprise as well.

"Babe, while I'm ecstatic that you love me, too, we should probably get off the ground." Blake pulled her up with him, and then crashed his lips on hers as the crowd clapped even louder.

"Oh, Blake, I love you so much." Tears fell down her cheeks and she could hardly breathe from the excitement of his surprise. "I'm so happy you came. I couldn't wait to jet back to St. Simons and tell you in person. I'm so happy you're here."

"Me too, beautiful. I had to see you."

"I missed you and I love you. I love that I love you," Reagan said, placing more kisses on his face. "How long will you be here?"

"My plane leaves tomorrow night."

"Where are you staying?"

"I got a room at the Peabody."

"So why are we still standing here?"

"Good question. Let's go."

Raven tossed Reagan her purse as Blake gripped her hand and led her out of the building.

Later on that night, Reagan laid nestled in Blake's protective embrace after they'd made love with her saying she loved him the entire time. She couldn't believe she was finally in a place of peace in her life. She'd finally forgiven her father and she'd fallen in love with a man who was patient enough to not let her insecurities cause him to leave her.

"I can't believe one moment I was playing golf—and losing by the way—and the next I was zooming to the Jacksonville Airport to surprise you and hold you in my arms."

"This entire week I've been kicking myself over suggesting a silly break. I was having withdrawals from trying to be strong and not call you except for those few times."

Chuckling, he shook his head. "Yeah, with those ridiculous questions about my parents' party. I was like yeah, she misses me and is going crazy just like me."

"Each time I called I wanted to scream out 'I miss you and I love you very much' but I wanted to tell you in person. I've been holding it in for such a long time. Honestly, I've been holding it in since we met. I fell for you the very moment I saw you."

"Really? Because that's when I fell for you. I love you, Reagan."

Flipping him over, Reagan straddled his lap. "You have enough strength to show me one more time?" she asked, grinning.

"Always."

Epilogue

"Girl, by far this is the best event we've ever thrown," Zaria said as she entered the tent on the beach in front of Reagan's house. "And your dad is here. How cool is that?"

Reagan nodded as she glanced around the intimate gathering of family and friends that she decided to throw since her father and Ms. Rhonda were in town for the week, along with Justin and his family including his newborn baby girl. Blake's parents had just returned from a three month tour of Europe for their honeymoon trip. Reagan and the Precious Moments Events crew were somewhat relieved that their busy summer wedding season had ended even though the fall season would be full. She couldn't be happier at the moment as she watched Blake, her dad, Justin, and Blake's brother-in-law, Jerome, play spades while the General and Garrett barbecued ribs, burgers, and seafood. Blake's nieces and nephews played volleyball in the sand and Brooklyn commemorated the event by snapping pictures.

"This is like a dream come true in a way. My dad and Justin approve of Blake. But not only that, I'm in love with him and that is truly the best feeling in the world. Now I know why you and Shelbi are always smiling."

163

"Well, maybe you'll be in the same boat as us one day."

"I am."

"Girl, no. I mean the marriage boat. I didn't toss you the bouquet at my wedding for it to go to waste."

"You know what, Z? I can honestly say I'd love to be in that boat someday, and thanks to Blake, I'm no longer scared of commitment and marriage."

Her eyes met his in that instant, as if he knew she was talking about him. He winked at her and proceeded to slam down a card which apparently was the winning hand as he and Jerome jumped up and did a victory dance. Clara joined Jerome in the dance. Reagan admired how they were such a fun couple. However, she couldn't help but notice that Parker and Cliff, who were seated together eating with Mrs. Harrison, yet barely spoke or looked at each other in the same loving way as Clara and Jerome.

"Here comes your man. I'm going to go check on mine and see if those ribs are done." Zaria bounced off as Blake approached.

"Hey, babe," Reagan greeted as Blake pulled her in his arms and kissed her forehead. "I guess you won the spades game."

"Yeah, but it was tough. Your dad and Justin are serious card players."

"Yeah, I see." Reagan's stare turned in Justin and her dad's direction. They were indeed having a great time together, and Reagan finally felt like her life was complete.

"Look who's here!" Addison shouted and zoomed past as she zipped toward the trail that led to Reagan's deck.

Reagan turned to see whom Addison was referring to and spotted Chase giving his baby sister a hug. Reagan immediately searched out Brooklyn, who snapped a picture of the scene and then pivoted in the other direction.

Placing her attention back on Blake, he grabbed her hand and led her toward the ocean.

"Where are we going?" she asked.

"Just for a little walk. I need a moment alone with my lady."

"I totally agree. I haven't had you to myself all day, but I'm glad our family and friends are having a great time."

"Glad you planned this little gathering. You know I was thinking about maybe you planning another get-together with even more of our family and friends. I spoke to your dad and Justin about it earlier and they were all for it."

Halting, she turned toward him as a wide smile slid across his face like a Cheshire cat. Her pulse raced faster than a cheetah running across the dry forest, but she wasn't going to get her hopes up—even though Zaria mentioning marriage earlier may have been a hint.

"Why would you need to speak to them about that?" she asked slowly as her legs began to turn into silly putty.

"Well, I needed their blessing to ..." Pausing, he knelt down on one knee and cleared his throat. He caressed her left hand and reached up with his free hand to wipe a tear cascading down her cheek.

Her hand flew to her mouth as the tears fell even more. "Oh, Blake."

"Reagan, I knew from the moment we met that you were the epitome of what I've searched for in a life partner, my wife, my best friend. When I fell for you even more, I knew there was nothing I wouldn't do for you. I love you more than I can ever tell or show you, but I intend to do my best for the rest of our lives together." He stopped to wipe more tears from her face and then pulled a black box out of his pocket. Opening the box, it displayed a three-carat, princess cut diamond ring.

"Will you marry me, Reagan?"

"Oh, yes. I will, Blake."

He slid the ring on her finger and rose to capture her lips with his in a passionate kiss that reminded her of the kiss they had on their first date. Something in her heart knew even then he would be the last man she'd ever kiss.

"I can't wait to tell our family and friends," she said, admiring the ring. "Oh wait. I have the feeling they already know."

"Nope. Not all. Just your dad, Justin, Zaria, and Brooklyn, who I asked to take pictures of the proposal."

"I can't wait to share the ..." She trailed off as she glanced down at her feet and the ocean water that covered her sandals and his tennis shoes all of a sudden. The tide had come ashore and a huge wave knocked them both over into the water.

Once they helped each other up, they ran up the sand and crashed down on it in laughter.

"We're soaking wet," Reagan said, laughing so hard her stomach ached. "Is it me or do we have a habit of falling over each other?"

"I think it's safe to say we're going to keep falling for each other for the rest of our lives, my lady."

"Perfect. I can't wait."

The End

Extras

Hi romance readers!

If this is your first time reading one of my books or you haven't read Justin and Shelbi's love story, check out the blurb and excerpt from *Cooking up Love* on the next page. It's my very first published book and the first book in the Arrington Family Series which is a complete series. Be sure to check out the other books.

Happy reading!
Candace

Blurb

What happens when a suave, handsome chef meets a cute, sassy food critic?

When Shelbi Arrington accepts a position as a food critic in the hopes of burying her medical career and foregoing her residency, the last thing she's searching for is love. However, that's just what the doctor ordered especially when she lays eyes on the handsome chef, Justin Richardson. While sorting out her secret conflict of continuing her medical career, she falls for his mouth-watering charm, leaving her hungry for anything he has to offer.

Justin is leery of doctors because a doctor's negligence caused his mother's death when he was twelve. He has put his focus and energy into his restaurant, which had been a dream he and his mother shared. Justin is immediately smitten by the cute, sassy food critic that has him cooking up different ways to please her appetite. But when things start to heat up, Shelbi learns of a shocking revelation that could extinguish the flame of their relationship. Will Justin be able to forget his pain and commit to the woman who has stolen his heart?

Excerpt

"This is so delicious. Do you think they'll let me have another one?" Shelbi Arrington asked the waitress at Chow Bella's Italian Restaurant after she took the last bite of the tiramisu, savoring every sweet, sinful taste of the delectable dessert her hips needed to stay away from.

The waitress gave a sneaky look around the restaurant, then leaned over and whispered to Shelbi, "I'll see what I can do." She winked and hurried to the kitchen.

Satisfied with the response, Shelbi placed the to-go bag, which held the rest of her uneaten lunch, on the chair next to her purse. She had a habit of leaving her doggie bags and made an effort to remember this one. Her uneaten portion would serve as lunch tomorrow. She took out her iPhone and typed a few notes before tossing it back into her purse.

Shelbi rested her elbows on the checkered red-and-white tablecloth, making mental notes of the patrons and the decor. A few wrinkled their noses, one couple called a waiter over in disgust, and a group of businessmen checked their watches as they waited for the check. A party of eight in the corner booth was being serenaded with "Happy Birthday" by the waiters. Her favorite scene was of a small boy talking louder than anyone else, yet his parents still conversed and neglected to quiet him. The customers seated near gave the couple frosty stares, but they never noticed.

The waitress returned with a small bag, which she set on the table along with the check. She winked, and Shelbi winked back. She eased the smaller bag into the larger plastic one and tied the handles into a tight knot.

"Ms. Arrington, here's the check. Your lunch is on the house, but the manager thought you may want it in case you need the information for your article."

"Thank you very much, Lizzie." Shelbi took the slip of paper from the black leather receipt holder.

"You're quite welcome, Ms. Arrington. I feel honored to have served a famous food critic," Lizzie said before leaving to serve another customer.

Shelbi laughed. As a contributing food critic for *Food for Thought* with *The Memphis Tribune*, she was nowhere near famous. Some of her articles were featured in the newspaper and on their website. Plus, she had a large number of followers on her personal blog, *Food Passions*, which she started during her undergrad years at Spelman, but she wasn't famous.

She pulled her last five-dollar bill from her wallet, as well as all of the quarters at the bottom, and placed the money on the table.

Checking her watch, she had five minutes to dash to the next trolley that would take her home to her loft apartment at Central Station. There, she could kick off her heels, sip a latte, and eat the other tiramisu—sure to go straight to her hips—and type the article on the Italian restaurant and the other one from a few days ago.

Once at the trolley stop, Shelbi realized she had given all of her quarters to Lizzie. She dug around her purse for some loose change or a dollar, but all she found were eight pennies, her checkbook, and a half-eaten bag of Skittles. It was a fifteen-block walk from the trolley stop to her loft.

She'd made the trip several times in tennis shoes with her jogging partner, but never in her sister's Christian Louboutins and a dress.

The red trolley stopped in front of her, and the door slid open. Unfortunately, it wasn't the trolley driver who had a crush on her and gave her free rides whether she had money or not. She hoped the driver would have pity on her.

"Good afternoon...um..."—she glanced at his nametag—"Mike. It seems I have given all of my change as a tip to the waitress a few minutes ago. All I have are these few..." She stopped to hold out her hand. "Pennies."

The driver tilted his head to the side and looked down at her hand. "All you gave the waitress was some change?" he asked in a harsh tone.

Stunned at his remark, as well as embarrassed at the line of people behind her groaning impatiently, Shelbi didn't know what to say or do. She checked her wallet, hoping she had a dollar hidden somewhere.

"Move it, lady!" a man behind her shouted.

"Hurry up!" a lady with a crying baby screamed.

"I have a slice of tiramisu you can have," Shelbi whispered. "Never mind." She turned to go before she said something rude, or worse, cried from embarrassment.

"I'll take care of it," a deep, concerned voice to her left said. A whiff of intoxicating cologne floated by as the considerate stranger dropped a one-dollar bill into the trolley's money slot.

"Thank you." Shelbi looked up to see a chiseled, handsome face, and a sexy smile that caused her breathing to stop. When their eyes met, an immediate rush of sensual excitement washed over her skin. She glanced at his hand that had just placed the money in the slot. No wedding ring, but it didn't mean he was single. A man as chivalrous as him probably had women chasing him all over Memphis.

"No problem." He placed his hand at the small of her back. "Let's go sit down." The warmth in his voice and his kind gesture made Shelbi forget about her embarrassing moment.

While on their walk, Shelbi assessed his at least six-foot-one muscular frame, curly yet wild black hair, and a fair complexion with a slight tan as if he had just come from the beach. He wore jeans with a rust-colored corduroy jacket and a cream T-shirt, perfect for the first day of fall.

Shelbi was used to the take-charge kind of guy thanks to her dad and her two overprotective brothers. However, the way the stranger glanced down at her, giving her a comforting smile, made her heart skip a beat or two and was anything but brotherly.

Once settled in their seats, Shelbi turned toward him and once again was blown away by his strikingly handsome face. Her breathing unsteady, she tried to concentrate on the woman holding a baby the next seat over. Instead, her eyes were drawn to the good-looking stranger with dark, thick eyebrows and a neatly trimmed mustache with a slight beard growing in. He was sinfully delicious. If he were dessert, she would've devoured him right then and there.

"Thank you so much for paying my fare. Where are you getting off? I can pay you back."

He chuckled. "Baby, its only one dollar, but did I hear you say you have a slice of tiramisu?" He pointed toward the to-go bag in her lap.

"Why yes, I do, and you're more than welcome to have it."

"I'm teasing, but it's nice to know you were willing to give it to me."

Their eyes locked on his last four words. A heat wave rushed over her at the thought of *giving it to him*. Shocked at her thoughts about a stranger, she tried to stay focused.

"Well, you saved me from walking fifteen blocks in five-inch heels." Laughing, she stretched one leg for him to see the heels on her shoes—well, her sister's shoes.

"Hmmm…very nice…um, shoes," the gentleman said followed by a wink and a slight biting of his bottom lip.

Shelbi raised her eyebrow as she caught his curious eyes perusing her toned legs before they settled on her face.

"So what's your name?"

"Shelbi Arrington. And yours?

"Justin Richardson."

"Nice to meet you, Mr. Richardson."

She froze when their legs brushed as the trolley turned a corner, unleashing goose bumps all over her skin. She pretended to look out the window to hide the heat she felt rising in her face. She'd experienced these types of emotions before, but never within a five-minute time frame. In a few more moments, she would be at home, even though she really wanted to ride the trolley all afternoon with the handsome Mr. Richardson.

"I haven't seen you on the trolley before. Are you new to the area?" he asked, studying her face carefully.

"I just moved downtown about four months ago. Before then, I lived in Nashville."

"What brings you to Memphis?"

"I accepted a job at *The Memphis Tribune* as one of the food critics for *Food for Thought*."

His thick, dark eyebrows rose slightly. "You're a food critic? Critique any good restaurants lately?"

"As a matter of fact, I have. I went to Chow Bella's for lunch today, and a few days ago, Lillian's for dinner."

He nodded. "So, did you like Lillian's?"

"I can't answer your question. You'll have to buy a newspaper or go online to read my article on next Thursday," she said, smiling at him.

"Witty and beautiful. I like that. But I'm sure there's something you did or didn't like about Lillian's."

Shelbi hesitated for a moment. She really didn't want to tell a complete stranger, even though he did just rescue her from embarrassment and sore feet.

"Well, I was quite impressed with the atmosphere, and the food was delicious overall."

"Overall? What was wrong?"

"Nothing really. A few things could've been better. The barbecue sauce tasted a little bland, even though it's supposed to be the chef's special recipe. It seemed store-bought, and they don't serve pork, but this is Memphis, for crying out loud. Where's the pig?"

"Um…well, maybe the chef wants to try a healthier angle. Pork isn't good for your system. It isn't easy for the body to digest."

"I'll remember your tip the next time I cook bacon."

"So…" He stopped midsentence as Shelbi stood.

"This is my stop," she said disappointedly.

"Too bad. I really enjoyed talking to you."

"Me too. Thank you so much again for paying my fare." She stepped off the trolley and hesitantly glanced over her shoulder to see the fine-looking man one more time.

About Candace Shaw

Candace Shaw writes romance novels because she believes that happily-ever-after isn't found only in fairy tales. When she's not writing or researching information for a book, you can find Candace in her gardens, shopping, reading or learning how to cook a new dish.

Candace lives in Atlanta, Georgia with her loving husband and is currently working on her next fun, flirty, and sexy romance.

You can contact Candace on her website at www.CandaceShaw.net as well as subscribe to her email list for updates, excerpts, and giveaways.

Books by Candace Shaw

The Arrington Family Series

Cooking up Love
The Game of Seduction
Only One for Me
Prescription for Desire
My Kind of Girl

The Chasing Love Series
(Harlequin Kimani Romance)

Her Perfect Candidate
Journey to Seduction
The Sweetest Kiss
His Loving Caress
A Chase for Christmas

Precious Moments Series

For the Love of You
When I Fell for You
Then There was You (TBA)
When I Think of You (TBA)

Free Reads

Simply Amazing (Arrington Family Series)
Only You for Christmas (Chasing Love/Harlequin's
website only)

Made in the USA
Columbia, SC
13 April 2018